Finding Flame
House of Xannon Book 2

Copyright © 2014 Melinda VanLone.

Published by: WrittenHouse Publishing, Rockville, MD

ISBN-13: 978-0-9887455-3-7

Cover Illustration: Carrie Osborne

Cover design and book layout: Book Cover Corner, bookcovercorner.com

VanLone, Melinda.

Finding Flame / Melinda VanLone

Visit the author website: www.melindavan.com

For David,
who still supports my dreams.

CHAPTER ONE

Macari stood on the edge of a cliff, toes stuck out beyond the lip, and contemplated the craggy rocks that tumbled down to a valley far below. A soft breeze played with her hair and full, white skirt. It deposited the scent of trees in her nose and teased her body forward. She teetered, spread her arms out for balance, and wrapped her toes around the lip of earth. Heart pounding, she licked her lips in anticipation. It was a long way down, full of jagged stones and trees. Above, blue sky streaked with pregnant clouds promising rain. In front, a nearly invisible whirlwind of power, stirred by birds with massive wingspans, the Shee. The Air Ancients flapped slow, steady beats, moving in lazy circles. Below, white buildings dotted a lush green valley like drops on green canvas.

She took in a deep breath of warm air heavy with the hint of rain and stepped off the cliff.

She plummeted for a few seconds, enjoying the freedom

and feel of wind as it rushed her face, the sound of her skirt as it flapped furiously, and the complete obliteration of everything else. Rocks lurched toward her. She stared at them through the tears brought by so much air in her eyes. When she could see the shadows of each individual crevice on every stone, she twirled and lightly danced into the Wind.

Macari drifted along the edge of the slow outer flow of the Corsaerie as she settled her heart rate and caught her breath. She rested for a moment and watched the path of Air, filled with the debris of thousands of thoughts, actions and emotions. It was the entirety of existence, tumbled and merged into the recorded history that formed the vortex of power with no beginning and no end. Air. Pure Air. *I love it here. So much life, so many people. All going and doing and seeing. Wish I could step into the scenes and really live among them. Stars, but wouldn't that be nice.*

With a sigh, Macari turned and let the flow carry her backward. She took a deep breath, focused her intent and power, and took a deliberate step forward. Her eyes watered immediately. Another step, and both eyes spilled over, watering her cheeks. One more step, and a scene opened up in front of her, a shimmering window into the past.

Within, she saw a woman with shoulder length black hair, athletic body, and obvious power. *Human, not daemon.* She catalogued the information as she searched the vision for more detail.

Emotion hit her next, a mixture of fear, determination,

shock. The woman held her hands out in front of her, energy pouring forward in an attack against something large, scaly, and not quite human. Confused, Macari peered closer. The creature looked twisted, and his power held an aura that didn't make sense. *What in the universe is that?* Possibly daemon, because of his claws and power, but definitely also human, judging from his body and clothes. He attacked the woman with a blast of fire that should have annihilated her.

Macari followed the power, expecting the woman to vanish. But she didn't. She'd deflected it somehow, and in return pushed water and air.

Enthralled, Macari watched the creature strike with a clawed hand so fast she almost couldn't track the movement. When he drew back, the claw dripped blood. He brought it to his scaled face and a two-pronged tongue snaked out to taste it. Macari gasped along with the woman, startled. Her focus dissolved. The scene wavered and vanished. She spun in place to face forward again, frustrated.

Stars blast it. What happened next?

She knew it was no good to even try to catch the vision again. The flow of the Corsaerie, even in the calmer outer region, rushed too strongly to catch a scene twice. Still, she could try to find a portion of what followed, if she acted fast enough. She turned in place, held her arms wide for balance, and stepped forward.

A new window appeared, revealing a meadow, surrounded by trees. A woman with dark hair stood with her back to Macari.

She squinted, trying to make out more. The woman turned slightly, looking behind her at something Macari couldn't see. *Found you!* It was the same woman. Macari's sense of elation at knowing the woman survived the attack gave way to concern. The woman's eyes swirled with emotions, and dark circles rimmed them as though she hadn't slept in weeks. Confusion, frustration, trepidation all wound their way around the vision.

What's going on? Another attack?

Macari looked past the woman to a dark haired man with vivid blue eyes. *Daemon. Mayfanata. Part of the Court.* She could tell by the black pants, black shirt, and attitude. He exuded confidence and secrecy. *Typical.* She focused again on the woman. A heightened sense of lust reached Macari and she grinned. *He wants her.*

The man took the woman's hands and the two exchanged energy, though the woman seemed on one level reluctant and concerned, and on another level incredibly excited. Conflicted. Macari watched for a few seconds, then released the scene. She didn't need to witness the climax. It was rude to intrude on the moment, even if they'd never know.

Macari drifted further into the stream as she considered the two scenes she'd just witnessed. *Just human plane stuff. Nothing important. Not enough for my report.*

She stepped with the flow into the next level of the Corsaerie, then the next. The closer to the center she stepped, the further into the past she'd see. Since the last two scenes had been very recent, she pushed further, hoping to get something older. Viewing human plane events never fully satisfied First Mother, and the Court had no use for them. Though the one that included a daemon might pique their interest, a simple energy exchange wasn't worth shouting about. She stepped deeper, going further into the Wind than she'd normally go, hoping for something more significant.

The Corsaerie roared around her, bombarded her with emotions, slapped her with thoughts, none of them coherent. She couldn't help but giggle her delight. It felt *alive*. To be a part of the flow meant to surrender and become one with something larger. Something *more*. *It's like feasting on energy or joining with the universe.* The colors of so many events pulsed, so vivid they hurt her eyes. She closed them to make it easier to lose herself.

In the chaos, a thought, clear and focused, drifted out of the onslaught. Not a complete thought, more like an intense longing. A need. A burning desire so strong it overrode everything around her. Whoever it was, and whatever it was they longed for, felt ancient and timeless. They'd been waiting around for something since time began. To want something that badly, for that long…

She latched onto the thought and emotion, curious to see if she could find out what it was he so desperately wanted.

Startled, she realized the pronoun was accurate.

Who are you?

Her need to know carried her along with the strands of ancient desire until the two fused. Something…some*one*…tugged at her, knocking her off balance. She slammed into the stream, unable to maintain control. Her attachment to the specific thought and emotion was like holding on to a piece of rope while someone dragged her through a tornado. She couldn't let go of the rope now that she'd grasped it. Wind pushed her through the whirling mass. Energy and power descended all around her and pressed close. She couldn't absorb this much, and she couldn't let go.

Tingles burned their way up her body, from her toes to the top of her head. Her skin felt as though it melted as the invisible rope she clung to dragged her unmercifully along a path she couldn't see, couldn't detect, couldn't change. Then a burst of light, a wrenching of cosmic energy so intense she nearly blacked out. She cringed, expecting a blow.

Stars take me!

A searing jolt of energy wracked her body. Macari gasped, tried to wrap a shield of air around herself, failed to form anything like it, and instead pushed out in all directions with it. She managed to spin until her back was to the flow. Immediately, another window opened in front of her. She hadn't expected it to, but the relief it provided from the raging storm was welcome. She huddled next to the window she'd opened, thankful for the release and a chance to catch her breath.

The view was limited, more vertical than horizontal, so she saw only a portion of sky and land. Deep forest in between. In the background, auras of power emanated from three or four sources. In the foreground, a large fire, and people. *Humans. Not recent, though. Clothes look primitive. So do the huts in the background.* They seemed unaware of the energy in the distance. They sang around the fire, and some sipped from bowls.

They're happy. She smiled, and looked closer at the people. A woman joined the group, hair and clothes dripping wet, a knife tied to one thigh, a smile on her face as she greeted a man who offered her a bowl. The tilt of her head, the way she turned toward him, made it obvious she liked the man. *She loves him. I bet they joined later.*

In the shadows of the trees, two bright specs of light glowed, flickered, flared again. *What is that?* From this distance, she couldn't tell. But she saw that the woman with the knife noticed it too because she stiffened and stared in that direction.

Movement to the left caught Macari's attention. The energy had drifted closer. She could make out individual shapes. Five of them. They hovered in air above the group, hands outstretched as they cast some sort of power. *Daemon. That's a lot of air weaving, to leave a trail like that.* She wanted to shout a warning to the humans, despite how ridiculous the idea was. There was no going back in time, no way to change what had already been done. But it didn't stop her from wanting to. Even though this obviously was so far back in the past it hardly mattered, she worried for the humans. *This is before the split. Daemon and humans together in the same plane.* She'd never seen a vision from before the split, and this one felt ripe with ominous undertones. The intent of energy didn't feel good or peaceful. It felt…oddly detached. Cold. Cruel. She cringed as power pulsed out from the daemon toward the humans.

Energy erupted over the happy group to form whirlwinds of destruction. Men and women ran, screamed, or huddled behind benches. Macari watched, horrified, as a group of larger men carrying sharp weapons ran into the middle of the camp. They struck seemingly at random, slashed at anyone within range. One of the villagers fell into the fire. Another gushed blood from a neck wound. A third tried to fight, but was met with a brutish mountain of a man who twisted the villager's neck and then tossed the body aside as though it were trash. Through it all, the daemon provided confusion in the form of dust storms, and what might have been shields that prevented escape to the forest.

Macari's gaze followed one woman as she sprinted past the bonfire in the opposite direction of the rest. Determination and anger etched lines on her forehead and put fire in her eyes. It was the woman with the knife, the one who'd been so wet. She passed through the vision window and out of sight.

Where are you going? What's over there?

Frustrated, Macari looked back at the bonfire. At the base of it lay the man who'd been eating with the woman. His throat had been slashed, an arm severed. The brutish invader lifted the body and tossed it onto the fire, which flared and licked hungrily at the remnants of what had been an innocent, peaceful human. Macari shuddered. She'd never liked fire. It felt dangerous and chaotic.

And deadly.

Macari backed away from the scene. The last thing she

saw, before she stopped the vision, was the five daemon. Their smug faces and outstretched hands. They obviously directed the invasion. She noted their long bodies and hair. Two, flowing white robes and pale skin, green eyes. Three, darker skin, blue eyes, black robes.

Daemon. Mayfanata. And Benata. Working together.

Horrified, she turned in place to close the window. Without that small buffer, the wind grabbed and pulled her viciously into the stream. She tumbled, unable to get her balance, her sense of up and down completely violated. Horror at what she'd seen interfered with her ability to focus and push herself out of the Corsaerie.

She closed her eyes, trying to block the memory, and spread her arms wide. Let the wind flow through her. Concentrated on the cliff's edge, the valley, and on stepping *out*. When she had it all firmly in mind she twirled and danced until she reached the edge of the Corsaerie and managed to somersault out into the blue sky. Thunder and the first drops of rain welcomed her home. She revolved in the air, suspended for a second, maybe two, before she plummeted. Treetops rushed to greet her, with ground right behind them. She thrashed, trying to stop the momentum before she met a tree face first.

CHAPTER TWO

As the ground yawned a welcome filled with the promise of pain and possible death, Macari curled in on herself and revolved, gathered power, and fashioned a cushion formed of Air that she shoved underneath her. She swore, a word in an old language rarely voiced but entirely appropriate, and relaxed into the cushion, which now brushed the top of a tree. Her heart pounded an unnatural staccato rhythm. Visions of herself lying in pieces on the rocks swam through her mind. She'd never lost focus like that. Ever. She'd never heard of an air daemon who died by falling from the sky, but she imagined it could happen if one were distracted enough.

That last vision had pierced not only her heart but her understanding of society. *Benata and Mayfanata. Together.* In her lifetime that had never happened. The two factions didn't even communicate. At all. Mayfanata City hovered on the eastern shore, and Benata City near the west. The Stulos formed a virtual wall between them, each faction remaining on their respective side. She stared at the Stulos now, lost in the memory of a scene so fraught with consequence she couldn't quite fathom the fullness of it. Within the torrent of Air that spun before her, she saw the bonfire and the humans as they ran screaming from the attack. She heard in the gentle flap of Air Ancient's wings an echo of the daemon's power as it rained terror on the innocent.

To have both factions not only working side by side but doing something so obviously evil repelled her. To cause harm to another living creature... *More than that, to murder...it's not the Benata way.* To the Benata, life was valued above all else, precious beyond measure. To take it...

She swallowed the lump in her throat. *It can't be real. Can it?*

Maybe power in the Corsaerie had twisted the vision. Shown her a fantasy. Or imagination, run wild. That had to be it. She clung to the thought, though it seemed a foolish delusion to pretend it was anything other than what she knew in her heart to be true. All of history lived on the Wind. It showed what was real, not things conjured out of overactive imaginations. Still. She had to find out if others knew about this event. *Mother will know. She'll know why too. Surely there was a reason. Something I couldn't see in the vision. Some justification.*

Filled with a sense of dread she couldn't explain and with the afterimage of the distressing scene burned on her mind, Macari let her focus on the Air cushion dissolve and traveled down to the edge of Benata City. She walked along the dirt path that formed the main passage between rows of white buildings on each side, rather than traveling straight to her destination. She needed to decompress. Let her thoughts calm. She couldn't step into the court building in this chaotic state. *First Mother won't like this overt display. I'll be late for my report, but surely she'd rather that than have me show up broadcasting.*

Emotions from other daemon bombarded her from both sides as she moved toward the center of the city. Everything from boredom to lust. Her talent absorbed every fluid piece of it. The emotions rammed into her brain and magnified. If she weren't careful, the resulting cacophony would spread to everyone around her.

Come on, Mac. You can do better than this. Lock it up. Lock it all up. Nobody wants to feel this. Stars, neither do I.

She stopped walking and closed her eyes, picturing a long corridor lined with doors. Each door led to emotions she'd absorbed but couldn't process. Feelings that threatened to overload calm, to claim her mind and destroy her place in society. She took her own horror and shoved it behind a door. The door refused to close.

She pressed her lips together and tried again with something easier, the lust from several buildings away as two daemon joined. Anger in the building next to her. Happiness further up the path. Each one went behind a door, locked safely away one at a time. At last she was able to wrestle her own horror behind a distant door within the corridor and lock it, though the barrier felt weak and threatened to burst. She continued down the path.

So many people. So much innocence destroyed. It can't be true. It can't be real. It can't be.

Her mind knew it was, but her heart couldn't bear it. She paused next to a tree not far from the court gazebo where she knew First Mother would be waiting and desperately tried to collect her thoughts. Ruthlessly she shoved each scene she'd witnessed behind a shield within her mind. She took deep breaths to still her pulse. Listened to the breeze rustling the leaves nearby. The gentle chirp of birds. The soothing sound of a fountain.

Those poor people.

She shoved the thought aside. She had a duty. She must report what she'd witnessed, no matter what the reaction might be. Knowing that such a nightmare scene was bound to stir controversy, she wondered if perhaps just this once she'd hide it from public view. It wasn't an easy thing to do inside the court building, but she could try.

Mother will know.

Which meant everyone would. Macari resolutely put one foot in front of the other toward the gazebo, determined to fulfill her duty no matter how painful. As she reached the entrance arch, she lifted her lips in a smile and skipped the last few steps, just to give her body the boost she'd need to make it past the report.

Majestic columns formed archways on all four sides and a lattice roof stretched overhead allowing the sun's radiance through. Growing things surrounded the building, as though it had sprung from the depths of a forest. The entire area had stood for thousands of years and was imbued with so much magical power that it lived, breathed, and allowed communication to happen in ways that weren't possible elsewhere. Inside the gazebo, all thoughts joined to become one mind. Without a strong personal shield in place, anyone inside the arches could delve into the thoughts of another. Not just mind-speak, but truly experience someone's innermost mental dialogue. It made solving problems an easy, fast discussion. But it also created them, especially if someone harbored bad thoughts against another. All lay bare, in the court gazebo. It was why most daemon avoided this place. If they didn't have to be here for official business, they made sure to have something to do far away from it. Always.

Bird song, rustling leaves, and the pleasant music of wind chimes filled the air. The scent of sun-warmed roses drifted with it. If the gazebo were empty, it all combined into an incredibly serene setting, and Macari didn't mind basking in the stillness. But the peace she usually relied on failed to touch her today.

As Macari passed under the arch and into the space, power crawled over her skin, raised the hairs on the back of her neck and burned into her mind. The connection to every person in the space formed next. The buzz of voices filled her head.

"First Daughter. You are welcome." First Mother's voice, ever present, rose above the others as the strongest, central speaker.

Others echoed the sentiment. The entire Court was already present and connected. Her mother wouldn't be happy that the report hadn't been given in private, but there was no turning back now. Macari smiled, stepped into the center of the space, and bowed her head slightly. *"Well met, First Mother. Well met, Council."*

She waited, wondering if perhaps her mother would skip the report until they were alone.

"Daughter. Please. Show us the wisdom you discovered on the Corsaerie today." First Mother spread her hands to indicate the gathered daemon.

Macari's stomach sank. A direct order, and one she had to obey, no matter the consequences and no matter how much she might resist. She slid back the outer shield in her mind to reveal the first scene she'd witnessed. Maybe she'd get by with only one scene today. The black-haired woman, being attacked by the odd lizard creature.

In her mind, mutters and conversations erupted.

"A Laghairtine? But they died out long ago."

"They appear to be reborn. The clothing on that woman suggests this is recent."

"She's not daemon."

"The human plane has Laghairtines?"

"How was this possible?"

One voice rose above the rest. *"Daughter, how far in the past is this?"* First Mother's tone put a stop to all other speculation, and everyone waited to hear the answer.

"Very recent, First Mother. This presented on the outermost edge of the Corsaerie. If she's human, I can't determine whether this was a star cycle or a moon shift. I don't think their passage of time is equal

to our own. But I don't think it was more than a turn past."

Several daemon shifted; two turned their bodies away from her. Anytime she mentioned her physical presence in the Wind it made them uncomfortable. The skill she possessed, unique among the Benata, reminded them of her other skill. The one that took their emotions and told her how they truly felt about things, no matter what their words might indicate. She felt shields push into place, though none successfully blocked any emotion. She felt their trepidation, concern, fear, and loathing as clearly as if they were her own. She took it all in, locked it away. The last thing she needed was to return the mix magnified. They hadn't seen the last vision yet. She wanted them all calm.

"Did you see anything else?" First Mother prompted.

With an inward groan, Macari slid back the next shield to reveal the second scene. The black-haired woman with a Mayfanata.

"She's human."

"A human joining with a daemon."

"Scandalous."

"It shouldn't be possible."

"How did they manage this?"

"Why are they joining?"

Voices filled with outrage shocked Macari more than the scene. Why they should care about an intimate moment between two strangers she couldn't fathom. What difference did it make?

"The difference, Daughter, is that particular Mayfanata is Ruarc,

their current leader. And he should not have the ability to communicate with the human plane. Balance has been breached, as well as Agreement. "First Mother tensed with barely contained anger. Macari absorbed it along with the rest of emotions, startled to discover her mother allowing such a heavy feeling to leak out. She'd never been able to detect her mother's emotions like she had everyone else's. The mother-daughter bond had enabled a natural shield between them.

Macari studied her mother, confused. *"If Agreement had truly been breached, wouldn't penalties have been called? We'd have heard the pronouncement, surely. And we didn't. So why should this matter to us? They're just exchanging energy. Something we all do."*

"She's human!"

"What was the result?"

"What happened next?"

"How did she get there?"

"Why did he meet with her?"

"What did he gain?"

First Mother held up a hand to silence the voices. *"Ruarc never acts without intention. Whatever the reason, we can be sure it benefits him directly and the Mayfanata as a whole. They obviously seek advantage over us, and this woman is the key. Her ability to cross the barriers is evident. I know that meadow, it lies on the edge of the Between but on the daemon plane. We must investigate how this was done. There could be a rift in the boundaries. The Stulos could be weakening. If it falls, our world will be destroyed. We may need to bolster it or strengthen defenses, but before we act, we must know more."*

Many voices echoed the decision. Concern turned to anger and a small amount of panic. Macari grabbed at it, shoved it behind doors in her mind automatically. She studied her mother, who stood stiffly erect with her hands clasped and eyes wide.

Instinct pushed her to dip a bit further behind her mother's shields, wondering why a simple joining would anger her mother this much. Before she managed to get any useful information, her mother turned on her. *"First Daughter, I sense there is more."*

Stars crash it. Macari bit her lip. She'd left herself vulnerable while she pried at her mother's private thoughts. *"Perhaps I should report the rest in private."*

Shock rippled through her mind.

"What could be worse than what we've seen?"

"Why the secrecy?"

"That is not the Benata way."

Disapproval from everyone made her flinch. She'd had enough of the negative overflow from two simple, inconsequential scenes. It was time she showed them something to be truly upset about. Ruthlessly she shoved aside the shield she'd wrapped around the last vision and let them all see the horror she'd witnessed.

CHAPTER THREE

As the scenario played out in her mind Macari braced for the storm of outrage sure to come. When the vision concluded, she watched and waited. While some shifted uncomfortably, no one reacted with anything stronger than curiosity. They seemed detached, and no horror or even concern drifted her way. The only thing she felt from the entire group was acceptance. As though the scenario had been nothing more than a story. Something that didn't matter. Something inconsequential.

She turned to her mother. First Mother's hands dangled relaxed by her side and her face had resumed its normal calm repose. *"Does this complete your report for today, First Daughter?"*

Macari nodded, confused. She listened as the group proceeded to dissect the vision in detail. *They act as crows on a carcass, feeding on gossip. They care more for one joining than they do for the murder of so many innocent humans. Murder, at daemon hands.*

She couldn't stop the mounting frustration nor could she hide it while connected with the others. How could they be so callous? How could they not care? Didn't they see? *What's to stop such an event from happening again?* She'd never seen such a thing on the Wind before, so the fact that it appeared today must mean *something. Maybe it was a warning or omen or maybe it hints at an evil alliance being formed even as we speak.* Frustration morphed into anger, tinged with fear. *How many others died then? How many will die in our future? Why don't you care?*

"Daughter." The sharp tone in her mother's mind touch dragged Macari out of contemplation. She'd been broadcasting the thought when she hadn't meant to. *"You will return to the Corsaerie at once. We must know more. What happened after this meeting? Is the woman now with child? Or has the child already been born?"*

Macari huffed, barely able to stop the string of curses poised at the edge of her mind. *"It's nearly impossible to find the same person again, Mother, let alone the next event. The windows are random, and the Corsaerie is constantly moving and changing."* Macari spread her hands. *"I don't know what happened next. I don't know why. What I do know is that daemon, at one point, were murderers. Air daemon. Mayfanata and Benata, side by side. Killing humans. If one woman could cross the plane, perhaps even more humans are being murdered as we speak."*

Her mother's face closed down. She clasped her hands tightly as she gave Macari a hard look. *"Let the past be past, Macari. We have more pressing issues. I'm much more concerned with the recent events you've shown us today. The Mayfanata move against us. You must investigate."*

First Mother turned her back on Macari and stepped through the crowd, gently touching arms here and there as she nodded, dismissing the Court. The assembly exited the area in twos and threes still talking, some out loud, some in mind-speak. Their voices left Macari's mind as they exited until she stood alone with her mother in the center of the space.

Macari frowned. *"I saw nothing that indicated they were concerned with Benata in any way. I saw one daemon joined with one human."*

"To what purpose?" First Mother turned to face her, the only daemon left within the mind net.

Macari spoke aloud, needing the emphasis she could provide with real sound. "The usual *purpose*. Enjoyment? Love? A boost of energy? Why are you more concerned with one joining than the murder of so many innocents?"

First Mother stiffened. "Macari. Whatever daemon did in the ancient past is of no concern to you nor anyone else. The past, as you've so often informed me after walking on the Wind, is written. We must concern ourselves with the present and the future, things which have not yet been written on the wind. Things we may be able to prevent."

First Mother's hands twitched as she spoke, a nervous tic seldom exhibited in the open. When Macari focused on the movement, her mother clasped her hands tightly behind her back. "The Mayfanata never act without benefit to self, therefore any action taken by their leader is suspect. He does not act for society's benefit, but for his own. This is what concerns me, and should concern you. He strives always to gain an upper hand. And you fail to mention one other reason for such an event."

Macari tilted her head to invite the answer rather than try to guess what was really bothering her mother.

"Procreation."

Macari had to strain to avoid rolling her eyes at the word. "Joining is a life affirming event and nothing more. Even if it resulted in a child, what possible harm could one *human* child do?"

"The possibilities are endless, daughter. You have not seen the depths of depravity to which one who lives in the Mayfanata way can sink. I hope you never experience it yourself. To that end, we need more information and you must gather it. Return to the Corsaerie. Find the sequence and discover what happened next."

Macari stomped a foot, rippling her skirt. "It can't be done. Can't, and shouldn't. Walking the Wind isn't like selecting items off a shelf. I can't simply order up a scene as I would a meal. It shows me what it wishes to show me, *when* it wishes. And this time, it wished to show me ourselves, Mother. This time it wanted me to know we are murderers. I'm much more concerned with why it chose to show me that. At first, I thought it couldn't be real. That I'd imagined it. But now I see that not only was it real, but perhaps it could happen again. History could repeat itself. Tell me, Mother, why did we work with the Mayfanata to kill humans? Is this something you would do again?"

First Mother pressed her lips together in an angry line. Her eyes flared. She stepped forward and whipped her hands around to clasp Macari's hand so fast she didn't even have time to draw breath. Her mother shook with barely suppressed rage.

And fear. She's afraid. Of what?

As she started to ask, First Mother silenced her with a tight squeeze and burst of power along the back of her left hand. *The heart line.* Her hand felt as though it had been dunked in ice water. A current of ice traveled up her arm to the center of her chest.

After the initial weave of power, First Mother spoke, the words so cold they forged a block of ice in the pit of Macari's stomach.

"First Daughter, by life bond and Agreement you are hereby issued a primary command. Seek the woman of your vision and determine who she is, whether that joining resulted in a child, and most importantly, why it was done. This you must do, no matter how far the journey. If you cannot find the information on the Corsaerie, then seek the human plane. If you return without fulfilling the mission, bond penalties apply. You have one star cycle to report."

With each word, needles of fire pricked Macari's skin. The stench of seared flesh wafted up from her hand as the binding burned itself into her soul. As the last word sounded, First Mother released her grip. Macari snatched her hand back and rubbed the sore spot. As she'd expected, the symbol for Air had been etched there, a black sigil against white flesh, surrounded by angry red burns. It would mark the time left to complete her mission as commanded. Each day it would fade a little more. When it faded away to nothing, time expired and the mission failed. Such a mark served as both a badge of office and a warning.

Macari clasped her hand over the mark and gaped at her mother, stunned. "You'd banish me for this?"

"You take your position too lightly, daughter. I asked, and you refused. Therefore, I must command. For the safety of the Benata, I must act. This information is vital to our existence. I will not have our society at risk because the First Daughter chooses to wallow in ancient history and forget her duty. Do as I command; abide by your Agreement." First Mother turned and stalked out of the court gazebo, their mind link severed.

CHAPTER FOUR

Macari stared at the mark on her hand. Her skin tingled and itched as the burn began to heal. She didn't know what to think. Her mother, usually so controlled, radiated fear and anger. It couldn't all be the result of the vision. She was sure of it. This fear had been old and deep, like a nightmare long buried in the subconscious. Something else lay behind the words. Some internal drive pushed this bizarre need to have information, and the fear of one human woman. *One woman, and maybe one child. What could they possibly do that would cause this reaction?*

The thought that perhaps she'd been partly at fault didn't escape her notice. She'd been so caught up in the horrible vision and the Court's lack of reaction to it that she'd let emotions slip out. Even her mother, usually so tightly shielded and with basic natural immunity to her daughter's talent, had to have felt it. Macari swallowed. The second she'd lost concentration on her mental shields, she'd sent panic and fear through everyone around her to the point that her mother now seemed paranoid about what had to be an innocent event. *Stars, I can't relax, not for a second. What if I'd lowered my shields completely?* She shuddered as she imagined possible reactions. *If anyone ever felt all that I've kept hidden behind locked doors, they'd explode with the overload.*

A headache bloomed behind her ears, and her stomach churned. The binding power invoked by her mother forced her to put one foot in front of the other. The Agreement, made when she'd gone through the naming day ceremony at sixteen turns, meant she had no choice. She had to move toward her commanded purpose or risk breaking the bond.

A wave of panic flowed into her stomach and formed a nervous knot as she thought of the penalty, which would be invoked if she failed to produce the desired information. She'd be disowned. Banished from Benata City. Court. A daemon with no place to call home.

She'd never contemplated breaking a command before. This was only the second real command she'd ever been given, and the first, to walk the Wind, didn't count. First Mother hadn't invoked the full power of the bond, then. Macari had wanted to do it, raced toward it with the eagerness of youth excited with the promise of adventure. The show of command had just been an excuse to force the other court members to let her do it in peace.

But this command was real. Permanent. Could not be revoked. And invoked penalties. Consequences. *Forty turns past my naming day, and she chooses this moment to assert domination.* It defied logic.

As the bond settled, Macari tried to still her racing heart. *I have to make some sort of plan.*

She left the gazebo and traveled back to the cliff. No matter how ridiculous the reason, she now had a mission to fulfill and a limited time in which to do it. She turned her thoughts to the problem. It wasn't possible to find the same scene twice. She'd been lucky to see even a portion of what happened next, and by now, all that happened around that joining was deep within the Wind, mixed with everything else that happened since. It was a mote of dust in a sandstorm. She'd never find another image of the woman, much less the events immediately following the ones she'd witnessed earlier. *It's not possible.*

Just because the task was impossible, it didn't stop Macari from having to try to accomplish it. She'd been given an irrefutable command. *Do whatever it takes to get the information requested, or be banished. Forever.*

The white buildings of the city merged into one blob as she let her eyes un-focus, reaching deep inside for some solution to the problem. If she couldn't find the rest of the scenes on the Corsaerie, then the only way to accomplish her mission would be to locate the woman wherever she existed now. Try to get to know her, or at least ask about her.

The human plane. How the stars am I supposed to get there?

It shouldn't be possible and yet her mother had tossed

the idea out there like it was fact. Like she *knew* Macari would be capable.

Why? How?

Overhead, the sun continued to float through the sky, oblivious to her dilemma. Below, Benata City life continued as well. The troubling thing was, from reactions during her report, she'd guess most of the inhabitants would agree with First Mother. They probably felt that Macari was being insubordinate. That she'd provoked the penalty bond. Deserved it. For the good of society.

The histories of her people explained the split of the factions as an effort to bring peace to everyone. A way of separating different philosophies and ways of life. Of cushioning the humans from daemon interference. So everyone could move forward in peace, and Balance. If the visions she'd seen were true, the real reason for the separation of planes lay in the murder of the innocent humans in her vision.

No wonder the Balance Court split the planes. How could any human have withstood that kind of power? They'd have been easy to slaughter. They WERE easy to slaughter.

Through one peek into the past, Benata City had become a stranger to her. Though every thought had been open to her, and Court had fostered an atmosphere of trust, underneath it all a sickness festered. They didn't lie, but they hid the truth. *And isn't that just as bad?*

Disgusted, she turned her back on the city to study the

Stulos. It remained strong and whole, supporting the planes and the space between. Had the splitting of planes really helped things? *Maybe.* Humans had flourished. While she couldn't spy on them directly, Macari had seen images on the wind over the years. Heard things. Their voices joined the storm just as daemon did. She'd admired the way humans used technology, how they seemed to get along without magic. The majority of scenes she'd witnessed offered no evidence that power existed at all, though every now and then a hint appeared. Like the black-haired woman, able to fight with water.

Surely we've changed. Benata now treasured life above all, society above the individual. They'd never go around slaughtering groups of innocent people.

If the split had been meant as punishment, a sort of timeout, then it had worked. Though she'd no idea how the Mayfanata functioned, she'd seen enough on the wind to know that wholesale killing didn't happen in their court anymore either. Though the way they passed leadership from one to another seemed a bit barbaric, involving some sort of fight to the death in a large arena. At least, it appeared that the loser died. Scenes never lasted long enough to be certain. Still. She'd never witnessed them killing a group of innocents, though they did seem to like to hunt animals.

It didn't make her feel much better.

Face it, Macari, it's not the horrible past but the horrible present that's bothering you. Your own mother just fed you to the wind stream without so much as a hint on how to accomplish the task. You're angry, even if you won't allow yourself to feel it.

Macari kicked at the ground, her soft shoes stirring up dust the wind whisked away. *Anger. It serves no purpose.* She locked it away. Glancing back down at the valley, she let her disgust and contempt for their attitude toward history ripple through the air to settle on the city. Satisfaction that at least for a few minutes they'd feel what she felt, even if they wouldn't understand why, lifted her spirits. Embarrassment quickly followed, which she suppressed. She shouldn't lash out like that. Not ever. *It's not like me. I'm better than that.*

Yielding to the inevitable, Macari spread her arms wide and closed her eyes, inviting the wind. It circled around her, pulling her hair, playing with her dress. She opened her mouth and breathed deep, ozone tickling her nose and the back of her throat. Then she slowly spun in place. Her body embraced the power of Air.

As it began to lift her, she danced. Her energy joined with nature, become one with the magic inherent in all living things. She felt the nearby Stulos, a deep black hole of power, pull on her. Entice her onward. She turned and stepped onto the outer edges of the Corsaerie.

CHAPTER FIVE

Instead of drifting along with the flow as usual, Macari continued to dance, twirl, and described a circle with her arms. She let the stream guide and shape her movement. The dance drove her deeper into the vortex, deeper into the clamor of voices, emotions, and images. Bits of conversation whipped by her ears, while vivid colors assaulted her eyes. Tears streamed down her cheeks and her skin tingled as though she'd fallen asleep. She closed her eyes, focusing on the one she wanted to see. *The dark-haired woman with Ruarc. Just the woman.* Her mind drifted to the horrible scene on the beach, but she ruthlessly pulled her thoughts back to focus on the more recent history.

The beach nudged her thoughts again, breaking her concentration. The woman in it seemed familiar now. Dark hair, like the modern-day woman, but definitely not the same era clothing. *Are they related?* Macari gave in to the impulse and, in her memory, studied the woman, trying her best to avoid looking at the slaughter. She remembered how the woman had smiled at her man. How her hair and clothes had been wet and then, suddenly, dry. How she'd run from the scene as the village burned and the people died.

Where did she go? What's to the left?

Macari huffed in frustration. She'd never know why the woman had gone that way, when everyone else tried to run to the forest or the huts or further up the beach. Why she alone chose that path. She'd never know if the woman lived, even, or if she'd been captured just out of sight.

She'd never even known the woman's name. The thought made her unaccountably sad, as though she'd lost a friend. *Silly. It's long past and not my fault.*

Something slammed into Macari's back and shoved her sideways. She lost her sense of balance and tumbled, head over heels, unable to right herself. She windmilled her arms, and pulled on energy to help stabilize her fall but couldn't stop the momentum. Her magic only seemed to speed things up, rather than slow them down.

Just when she thought she might revolve forever, she rolled out of the stream and into a dead space forming some sort of calm eye in the midst of the storm. Wind suddenly gone, she nearly fell through the other side of the emptiness but managed to push at it with enough power to stop just in time. She opened her eyes, and saw the detritus of the wind circling all around her. Above, blackness dotted with a million bright points of light. Below, a funnel of time. She drifted in the middle, untouched and breathless.

She pulled hair out of her eyes and licked her lips. *Now what?*

She'd reached the center of the Corsaerie. Momentary elation segued into trepidation. She'd never been this far into the Wind. Had no idea how to get back out, though in theory she could simply dance out the way she always did. Could she view history here, in the center? Perhaps a specific point of history? Her pulse raced at the thought. This eye of the storm might be the answer to her problem. She might be able to complete her mission after all. *One way to find out.*

Macari gently pulled energy from the surrounding power stream and merged it with her own. When she'd gathered more than she needed, she paused. Usually, she'd simply step into the stream to open a window to the past. That wouldn't work here. Instead, she'd have to pull the stream to her. *Or open a window and hope.*

She thought about it. *If I try a viewing near the stream, it might work.*

Putting thought to action, she wove the waiting power strands into a window just at the edge of the calm center, where it almost touched the flow. She'd never guided the Corsaerie. Didn't really think it was possible. *No harm in trying.* She focused on the woman with black hair as she created the window. Tried to picture every detail of her, from the tilt of her lips as she looked at Ruarc to the fierce determination when she'd fought the Laghairtine.

When the window finally formed, at first it showed only wavering nothingness against the backdrop of history. Then, slowly, a picture emerged,

In the window, an older woman knelt on black sand surrounded by craggy black rocks. Gray painted her long black hair, but her fingers were nimble as she worked on an uneven piece of cloth. *The same woman? But older?* A surge of excitement quickened Macari's pulse. *She lived! This has to be her. It has to be.*

The woman wore a rough brown fabric skirt and tight leather-like top, just as she had before, with a short knife tied to her thigh with rough rope. The cloth in the woman's hands flapped in the breeze. A hint of sea salt whipped through the air around Macari. She'd never received scent on the Wind before.

It has to be her. She moved. She lived. She lived! Why it made Macari so happy she didn't know, but it did. She smiled as she watched, heart thumping in her chest, happiness leaking out past all of her shields to fly in the Wind.

The woman held one hand hovered over the cloth on her lap. The hand glowed with obvious power. Acceptance drifted through the vision and out to the Wind.

As Macari watched, the woman looked up as though she sensed a presence. She stared right at the spot where Macari hovered. Unsure if she could be seen, Macari waved.

The woman frowned, and tilted her head. Her face, darkened by sun and lined with age around her eyes and mouth, featured eyes full of worry and wisdom.

She knows I'm here.

A sense of longing invaded her psyche then. Overwhelming ache and need for something or someone. *The woman? What does she long for?* Confused, Macari studied the image. *It's just an image. That's all it's ever been. A window to the past. So why does it look like she can see me? Who is she?*

A tear crawled down the woman's cheek. She stared at Macari as if lost in thought, then bent over the cloth again. After a moment, her hand stopped glowing and she stood, the cloth in her hand.

She took slow, deliberate steps toward Macari. The woman held the cloth up, letting the wind wave it around, a delicate hold on one corner of it. She let go, and the wind took it. The woman watched for a moment, her gaze locked with Macari's. With a final nod, she turned and walked away slowly.

Macari watched as the cloth traveled the wind toward her window, then without any logic slipped through to join the vortex. The vision of beach and woman closed in on itself, chaos taking it away and mixing it with the rest.

What happened to the cloth? What was it?

Macari reached out into the stream, thinking only of the cloth. When something soft hit her hand she grabbed it and pulled. It took all of her strength to rip it from the rush, but when she was finally able to pull her hand back she held the strip of cloth in her hand.

Feeling triumphant, she clutched it tight and grinned.

The eye of the vortex collapsed and swallowed her in a tornado of power, voices, emotions so intense she burst into tears as it obliterated every thought, her will stolen, leaving her overloaded. She faded into the black night dotted with stars, clutching the cloth.

An eternity later, Macari drifted, tangled in the Corsaerie, uncertain how long she'd been there. Her body spun, but her mind calmed. She stared up at blackness so vast, so all encompassing, she could think of nothing. Feel nothing. It would swallow her whole, and nothing else mattered.

In the blackness, a million flecks of white light speckled and danced. She watched them. It was like floating in the night sky, except she knew this wasn't nighttime, and she wasn't at home. Panic flared at the thought that there existed no air to breathe. She squashed the alarm. Clearly, she didn't need breathable air. Something else worked here, something far greater than anything she'd ever encountered. This wasn't the Corsaerie. It was…more. The absence of Wind. The absence of everything.

Or, perhaps, the combination of all.

She stared at the pinpoints of light, and wondered if there was something she should do. Something she'd been sent to find. Something…important. One of the dots of light joined another, and another, picking up more light as it moved toward her.

Macari stretched out a hand, thinking if it just came a bit closer she could touch it. And if she touched it, maybe this would all make sense.

The light formed a blob, which raced toward her and stopped just out of reach. The blob stretched, and sparked, and coalesced into a large white bird that circled around her in graceful push of wing. The bird circled Macari several times, each revolution pushing Macari back toward the Corsaerie, away from the inky black night. She rejoined the flow, cushioned from impact by the gentle movement of the bird. The creature hovered in front of Macari like a hummingbird, though the wings no longer moved. It shivered, then morphed into the shape of a girl, dressed all in white, with white hair, white eyes, white translucent skin through which Macari could see twinkling stars. The girl brought with her the scent of jasmine and a feeling of curiosity and concern. Macari watched her in awe, knowing who, or rather what, it must be though she'd never seen this form of the creature before. *Shee?*

"It is not wise to take from the wind that which you did not carry in." The girl sang in mind-speech and pointed at Macari.

Macari glanced down at her hands and discovered she still clutched the cloth. It was real, the rough fabric brushing against her skin. *"She gave it to me. The woman on the beach."*

"She gave to the wind." The girl countered, and twirled, circling Macari several times before she stopped. *"She of Water. A token. A prize. A danger."*

"A danger? How do you know?"

The girl smiled. *"All that has been is written on the wind, Macari."*

"It's not…" Macari stopped, realizing she didn't know what to

call the Ancient. "You know me? You know my name?"

"We guard the Stulos. We are Air and Wind. A Walker touches Ancient even in passing, and in touching leaves a piece of herself."

"Do you have a name?"

"We are all names."

"So I can call you anything I want?" Macari tilted her head. The scent of jasmine surrounding the Ancient made her smile. *"You look like a Jasmine. You smell like one too."*

The Shee dipped her head slightly in acknowledgement of the name, then pointed at the cloth again. *"Caution, young Wind Walker. It is not wise to take from the wind."*

"It's not like I can put it back. It's here now. She gave it to me for some reason. What's the harm in figuring out why?"

Jasmine started to dissolve.

"Wait! I have so many questions. Please, wait."

Jasmine giggled and continued to dissolve, now more mist and stars than girl or bird.

"Who was that woman? Do you know her name?"

As Jasmine dissipated into the wind, a word sang on the breeze. *"Serin."*

Serin. The name sounded familiar, but Macari couldn't place it. She studied the cloth in her hand. Rough, with various shades of brown. Nothing special about it. Loosely woven, as if by hand. She turned it over in her hands. Nothing on it, no marks, no colors. Just fabric. She closed her eyes and let her power flow into it, testing, tasting it. It held…something. A distant taste, like salt.

A faint hint of more. Thoughts, jumbled. Feelings, scrambled. Macari shook her head and opened her eyes.

Why did she throw a piece of fabric at me? What was she doing to it?

Jasmine had called her water. Serin's abilities must have been focused mostly on water. *Which explains why I can't tell what's on this.* She'd have to find someone with water abilities to tell her what it meant.

The Water Ancients could cross the planes but they existed deep in the oceans. Macari couldn't go there, much less converse with them. Anyone with innate water abilities who wasn't an Ancient would be on the human plane. Right now, the human plane might as well be on the other side of the moon. She'd no idea how to get there.

So far, her attempt to do as First Mother commanded had left her with nothing to report. She couldn't go back until she had more information. And finding that information here in the Corsaerie was impossible.

I have to get to the human plane.

Her shoulders slumped with the hopelessness of the task. She caressed the cloth, and released the feeling of failure out into the Wind.

CHAPTER SIX

Macari's disappointment morphed into fear that her mother's command would be impossible to fulfill. *I'm probably already doomed to banishment. I'll never get home. I'll drift on the Corsaerie forever. Alone.*

Every court member took the binding oath and Agreement, but as far as she knew, no one had ever been banished because of failure to fulfill a command. How ironic that the First Daughter would be the first.

Why'd you do it, Mother? What frightened you so badly that you'd sacrifice your only child?

Macari let sadness out next. She couldn't stop the feeling of betrayal and didn't want to lock it up. Next came anger, at herself for letting her own emotions affect her mother's actions, and at her mother for reacting the way she had. It made no sense, but that didn't change the fact that the action, once taken, could not be rescinded. The mark on her hand pulsed as a stark reminder.

After she'd spent the last of her anger, Macari felt drained. Exhausted. It took a lot of energy to Walk the Wind, and still more to maintain the shields holding every emotion absorbed from others. She could let them all go here, but what good would it do? It wouldn't get her any closer to her destination. Wouldn't help find her way to the human side, nor show her scenes she desperately needed to see. The Wind could not be commanded or controlled. The Wind *existed*. It was for the walker to bend her body, mind and soul around it, not the other way around.

With the cloth gripped tightly in one fist, Macari spun in the Corsaerie until she faced the direction of the flow. It moved fast here. She stepped with it and tried to keep her body upright as she moved. *Like trying to walk on shifting sand in a tornado!* As she grappled with her body, she focused on the problem. She needed to find that woman, one way or another. If she couldn't force more visions, then she could use one of the visions she'd already witnessed as a destination for travel. *Maybe.*

She went over them one by one. The two featuring Serin were too far in the past. The places might not even exist now, and travel to an uncertain destination could result in disaster or death.

The attack on the black-haired woman hadn't shown her enough of the surroundings to travel. The meadow where the woman had joined with Ruarc was clear and fresh in Macari's mind. But it was still on the daemon plane. *I need to go to the human side. I need to find her.*

Knowing it was foolish, knowing that to use a moving target for travel could result in disaster, Macari nevertheless pictured the woman with black hair down to the last detail she could remember. The blood dripping off the woman's arm. The way she'd looked with Ruarc. Her confidence and trepidation.

How do I find you? Show me where you are.

The desperate wish flashed away, a lost spark of hope in a whirlwind. She didn't expect any response. As the only Walker, she knew there was no one to hear her plea. She didn't expect help from something as unfeeling as the pure Air that formed the Corsaerie.

The next moment her body slammed into a wall of emotions so fierce, so chaotic, they threw her sideways against the stream and once again into an uncontrolled dance.

Macari raced along the inner reaches of the Corsaerie in frantic revolutions. The emotions that breached her psyche formed a grip so tight she couldn't breathe, couldn't think. Her talent immediately siphoned them inside, where she instinctively tried to lock them away behind the appropriate closed doors just to ease the pressure. Longing. Desire. Yearning so deep it ripped her heart and soul. It felt ancient, as though an eternity had been spent within the confining walls of despair.

It had to be coming from someone, *something*, powerful. She'd never felt anything like it on the Wind before. This consciousness wasn't simply drifting through a vision of past events. Whoever was responsible for this had ripped holes in the Corsaerie where none should be. Her head pounded with the effort of intake. She couldn't hold this much. She struggled to maintain her position, to move out of the current, to close her mind safely behind shields, but it was no use.

Desperate, Macari focused on the one scene she could safely use for travel. Ruarc, and the black-haired woman, in a meadow. She spread her arms wide, letting the Wind and emotions rip through her. Taking a tiny portion of the energy flow, she tied it to her own and then *pushed* into the Wind, the meadow firmly in mind.

She felt herself fall, the wind roaring in her ears as her body dissolved down, down, down.

Macari landed flat on her back on something spongy with a thud, the breath knocked out of her. She choked out a cough, unable to do much more than wheeze.

That was graceful.

Grass poked at her legs and scratched her neck. Odd sparks danced in the air. Soft breezes played with her hair. She saw trees nearby, smelled grass and fresh earth. The meadow, just as she'd pictured it, extended around her in a broad circle that ended in tall trees. It was peaceful. Beautiful.

And wrong. Very wrong. *Something's missing.*

Sound.

No bees, no birds, and she couldn't even hear the leaves rustling in the wind. Confused, she turned around, inspecting the rest of the meadow. She couldn't see anything beyond the first level of trees.

This can't be the human side. Surely there'd be more life to it. Animals. People. Something.

She continued circling, taking a spiral circuit outward in search of a path, or anything else that would indicate where she'd landed. After a few revolutions she stopped and stared up at the sky. Bright, as though it were midday.

No sun. No sound. This...

To be certain, Macari tested her power by trying to create a loose weave of air. It should have been enough to move her skirt. Nothing. She couldn't access power at all. She knew exactly where she must be.

The Between.

Macari felt again for power, and again came up empty. *This isn't on the daemon plane. If it were, I could use my power. Mother was wrong. This meadow is not on the daemon side. It's in the Between.*

Since she could walk the Wind, it made logical sense she could end up in this place, even if most daemon couldn't. But it made no sense at all that a human woman landed here. Macari turned in place, looking for the exact spot where Ruarc had joined with the woman. She stopped abruptly when she saw a dark shadow standing near the trees.

The man drew her attention by doing nothing. He stood. Watched. His eyes burned as they studied her.

She squinted to get a better look. Her mind must be playing tricks on her. Nobody's eyes could toss flames around like that.

"Is this your meadow?" She shouted to him. She couldn't

sense anything about him. His power didn't flow on the Air for her to taste.

The man's gaze flicked down her body to rest on her hands. Macari brought them up protectively to her chest, and his gaze followed their movement.

"Who are you?" The way he just stood there, staring at her breasts, was unnerving. From this distance it was hard to see his features, but he had a fine male form—broad shoulders, long legs, dark hair, eyes that…she squinted. Was that really fire? An image of fiery eyes in the forest behind Serin flashed through her mind.

An echo of the emotions she'd taken from the Wind rippled through her. Longing. Despair. Her consciousness tried to soak them up and lock them away, but the absence of power made that impossible. A small battle took place, during which she thought her head would burst from the pressure. Finally, the emotions departed, leaving her with a headache and sense of loss.

I don't belong here.

"No, you do not." The man's voice, deep, and a bit creaky, reached her as though he stood right next to her. Flares shot from his eyes up into the atmosphere and disappeared.

Macari blinked. *Surely I imagined that last part.*

"Who *are* you?" She took a step forward, then stopped. It might not be a good idea to stand too close to someone with eyes on fire.

The man walked toward her, reaching her side in the time it took her to blink. Startled, she stumbled back a step or two, before she managed to make her feet stay in one spot. She straightened her shoulders and faced him. From this distance, his eyes seemed more human. The fire more like bright swirls in deep black eyes. Hypnotic red, blue, orange swirls that threatened to suck her in and lead her…where? She shook her head and blinked to clear his hold on her.

"Neat trick. I amuse you?"

Some emotion flicked through his eyes and was gone before she caught it, though she'd have sworn it was surprise. His gaze drifted to her chest again.

She glanced down. "Never seen breasts before?"

The man reached out a hand, and power flowed around him through his fingers and out around her, settling near her chest before snapping back.

That he could call power when she couldn't sent a wave of fear up her spine.

"What do you hold?" He continued to stare at her chest. Or rather, her hands, she realized.

"Nothing." She shifted her hands down and behind her back, keeping the cloth tightly wound in them.

The man glared. "What do you hide?"

It took all her willpower not to cross her arms in front of her chest or just throw the cloth at him and run. His eyes scared her. Dangerous. Uncontrolled. And longing, which speared a hole in her heart.

He's definitely not daemon.

Amusement flittered across her awareness again.

"Stop that. If you want to talk to me, then you have to talk out loud. You have no right to be in my head. I have shields up. Or did. It's not polite."

"You do not belong here."

She narrowed her eyes. "It was you, wasn't it. On the Corsaerie. I felt you."

"You disrupt Balance."

She noticed the man kept his gaze trained on her arms, as though watching for any sign of movement.

"My balance is just fine." Macari instinctively reached for her power, blinked when she hit the wall of nothing. Settled for searching her memory for clues. The spark in his eyes, more than anything else, told her exactly what he was.

Fire.

Which told her, essentially, *who* he was. She tried to test the air for his power, but ran into solid nothing again. Her energy lay dormant inside, with some sort of wall around it that prevented her access. Not gone, but unavailable.

He's blocking me.

The man shook his head. "The Between is all things and nothing. All elements, in balance."

She frowned up at him. "Who *are* you?" Though she thought she knew the answer, she wanted him to say it. Just in case.

The man tightened his lips. He seemed to be considering, his eyes a window to a thousand emotions and thoughts. Finally, he answered. "Lasair."

CHAPTER SEVEN

Macari searched her memory for all she knew associated with the name Lasair.

Fire Ancient. Assigned to the Between to maintain Balance between the planes and to ensure the Stulos remained solid and whole.

"Oh." He'd been here, in the Between, since the planes had separated.

A long time.

"An eternity." Despair laced the words.

It rebounded around Macari's head and back out. She stumbled as it exited, nearly tripping as though the ground shifted out from under her feet. Lasair steadied her with a firm hand on her arm.

"To attempt to control chaos is foolish."

Macari moved the fist that hid the piece of cloth subtly away from Lasair's steadying hand. "I'm not controlling anything. Not lately."

Lasair pressed closer, his eyes seeking hers. "The prison formed around you is your own design, young daemon. The mind is not meant to be caged."

The intensity of those eyes filled her with a sudden urge to run, but she stood her ground.

His gaze shifted to her hands. "You bring a message for me."

"Message?" She gripped the cloth tighter.

Lasair let go of her arm to point at the hand holding the cloth. "It bears my mark."

Since hiding it didn't seem to be doing anything, Macari spread the cloth out in her hands. "I see no mark on this."

"You look, you do not see." Lasair's fingers twitched, as if he itched to snatch it from her hands.

She turned it over, seeing nothing but rough fibers and a hint of green. No markings of any kind. But in the Corsaerie, she *had* felt something when she'd taken it. The look on Serin's face when she set it free lingered in her mind.

Lasair stiffened as though he could see the woman's face, as if it hurt him as much as a physical blow. Macari stared up into his eyes. His face, a tight mask, his eyes, swirls of red, orange and blue. "Serin." The word, barely a whisper, carried with it an intense longing that forged tears in her own eyes.

She blinked and looked away. The power of this Ancient frightened her. The Shee, while their energy far outstretched any she'd ever sensed, never felt this forceful, this dramatic. Chaotic. Lasair was an explosion waiting to happen. A volcano, poised to erupt and destroy everything in its path. But he was also trapped, a prisoner in the Between, contained for more lifetimes than she could imagine.

I'd go insane, trapped like this.

"Name your price." Lasair's voice, gravel over hot coal, sent a shiver down her spine, one filled with longing and something far more powerful.

"You loved her." She might as well have slapped him. He flinched. Closed his eyes, a soft sigh escaping his lips. He said nothing. He didn't need to. "You know this can't bring her back, right? She's gone. Long gone. All I saw was a fragment of the past, held on the Wind. Nothing more."

"Name. Your. Price."

Confused, she opened her fist to reveal the piece of fabric. "There's nothing on it." She examined both sides before looking up to find him staring at her, his eyes a hypnotic twirl that she might get lost in forever. She looked away again.

Lasair growled, a sound not unlike the purr of a cat, but more menacing. He pointed at her hand. "You bear a mark of binding. If it is why you journey, I offer assistance."

Macari shrugged, trying to ease the stiff muscles along her neck and shoulders. "I'm not sure you can help me. You're trapped here." She peeked at his face and looked away before his eyes could hypnotize her again. "And my mission doesn't involve anything in the Between."

"Name your price." His voice, softer, soothed her nerves

and promised something she didn't think she'd ever find here or anywhere on the Corsaerie. Hope.

Nice trick. He plays with emotions too. She thought about that, and about why she'd come here in the first place. Perhaps they could strike a deal. She had something he obviously wanted. If it was in his power to help, it might be worth it. After all, the cloth meant nothing to her, though the idea of letting it go didn't sit well. For some reason, it *meant* something. She wouldn't give it up without something equally valuable in return.

She pondered what she could ask for that might measure up. Deals carried the weight of power, and bad wording caused more havoc than anything else. For an Agreement, the wording mattered far more than the intent of the deal.

She considered her words carefully before responding. First, she needed to know if he could even help with her quest. Then she'd consider the wording of the Agreement itself. "I'm looking for a human woman, black hair, blue eyes, who met with the leader of the Mayfanata in this meadow." She hoped there hadn't been more than one. The description was vague, but to augment it, she pictured the scene in her mind.

Lasair blinked, the lids moving slowly down to hide eyes that briefly sparked blue, then back up to reveal pupils so dark they hid the swirls. For once, Macari could stare into his eyes and not feel hypnotized.

"You know who she is, don't you?" She tilted her head, considering. "Do you know if she lives? Is she with child? Do you know how long ago she stood here?"

"Time is not relevant."

"It is to me. Do you know the answers?" She could still feel the drag of her mission, even here in Between. She wasn't sure third-party information would ease the compulsion. Somehow, it seemed doubtful. Her mother wanted a firsthand account. "Can you help me find her?"

Lasair shifted, his gaze on the cloth in her hand. "Agreement can be reached. Though the way will not be easy."

To tell him she had no choice would be foolish this early in the process. Macari pressed her lips firmly together to stop any errant words from escaping as she thought about what she truly needed. *A way to the human plane. Some clue as to who the woman is and where to find her. And a way home once my mission is complete. Three parts.* It would make for a difficult negotiation, and she shuddered to think of what penalties would apply.

She turned her attention to Lasair again. He remained solid, a statue, like someone who had a lifetime to wait for a decision. He had no urgency. And the only thing he appeared to want was a scrap of cloth she'd taken from the Wind.

The exchange hardly seemed even. A bad sign.

Lasair's swirling eyes softened as he waited for her to sort her thoughts. He probably understood how desperate she was to complete her mission, and no doubt knew what lay behind it. *Why shouldn't he? He's an Ancient. It's not like I can shield my thoughts here. And he's obviously not above snooping.*

His lips twitched. "Name your price, Naoise Sha'Macariah." His words eased into her, soft, low, seductive.

She felt naked. He knew everything about her, and she knew nothing about him. The advantage was all his. The negotiation wouldn't be fair.

Fine. But just because you know about me doesn't mean I have to deal. I need to know who she is and where to find her. I need a way into the human plane, and a way home when my mission is complete. Are these things you can provide?

Lasair blinked, his eyes once again a rolling swirl of flames that sparked as she stared. Like watching a candle, mesmerized. She couldn't look away, didn't want to. He blinked again, and his eyes returned to a deep, black, fathomless pit.

Macari gasped. How long had she held her breath? It felt like something momentous just happened, yet they remained exactly where they were and the meadow remained unchanged.

"I offer this." Lasair held out a hand. Resting on his palm was a small, black stone, with red and gold veins running through it.

"A rock?"

Lasair's eyes flickered, the black briefly disturbed as if an internal fire were stoked by an invisible hand.

"You'd give me a rock, for this?" She waved the cloth.

"Do you agree?" He almost growled.

"You're not like other Ancients, are you?" She watched for any reaction. "The Shee don't have conversations like this."

Lasair's eyes flashed. "Do you agree?"

"Stubborn, too. You're more human than I'd have thought an Ancient could be."

"Human. Daemon. Ancient. All of existence shares a beginning and connects to the same power."

Macari shook her head. "No. Ancients have more. Longer lives. Immortal, basically. They're the building blocks of magic, the cornerstone of existence. Yet…you don't act like one."

"Do you agree?" Lasair's hands clenched into fists. The muscles in his upper arms tensed, bulged.

How is a rock going to solve my problem?

"I need to understand exactly what you offer."

"I offer you an artifact, daemon *child*. If successfully bonded, you will be able to travel between planes at will."

Macari blinked, stunned. *The Fire Artifact,* a legendary object, one that hadn't been seen since the split. And now she knew why. *He's held it all this time.*

The only artifact she'd ever seen up close was the Air Artifact, and that wasn't even whole. It was missing a central portion, a key, so its power wasn't complete. It had never been used that she knew of, not since the split.

"What do you mean, if?"

"The artifact responds to the one who bonds."

"What will it take to bond?" She stared at the stone in his hand. It seemed small, a lump of black. Insignificant, though she knew it wasn't. *Not if it's an artifact.*

"Like chaos, it cannot be controlled and chooses its own path of destruction or creation. It cooperates with the one who bonds, and will bond with one who is open, who fully accepts in return."

Macari raised her gaze to meet his. "Fully accepts." *What does that even mean?* It seemed easy enough. Accept the stone, bond with it, and getting to either plane wouldn't be an issue. Two problems solved.

Lasair's eyes fastened on the cloth. He didn't look up as he said the words. "Do you agree?"

"We need full terms. I will give to you this cloth, and in return you will tell me the name of the woman I seek, give me the artifact, and show me the way to the human plane." Macari hesitated. She could see a huge hole in the Agreement and no way to fix it. "What if it won't bond with me?"

"Then it will seek another."

"So that's my penalty? If I don't bond with the artifact, I'll lose it *and* my way home." To complete her mission, she needed his help to get where she needed to go. But it would do her no good at all if she were to get stuck there, unable to report back. As soon as she stopped moving forward with her mission, the life bond penalty would kick in and she'd be banished anyway.

"Anything worth having is worth sacrifice."

"I still don't understand why you're doing this. The Fire Artifact, for a piece of trash."

"Understanding is not necessary. Do you agree?"

"But without understanding, an Agreement is foolish. Deadly, even." She returned his gaze with one equally fierce. "Do you intend destruction?"

"Destruction is creation, daemon. I do not seek to take life. I seek to earn it." His words carried a wealth of hidden meaning, an undercurrent of determination and, for the first time, a spark of hope.

What do you hope for?

She had the feeling the answer to her question was vital on a large scale. A being this powerful, this ancient, this dangerous… for such a creature to have hope in something could mean the end of everything. *Or the beginning of something special.*

In her experience, there was only one emotion stronger than hope. And hope, in her lifetime, had always been a positive emotion. Something linked with love, happiness, desire. Hope provided energy when there was none.

"What do you hope for, Lasair?" She whispered the words, not sure he'd answer. Not wanting to make him angry at this stage of the negotiation. They'd both lay their desires in the open, which made this part of the deal the most vulnerable to interference or dissolution.

Lasair closed his eyes. He waited so long to respond that she'd nearly given up. When he opened them, they'd changed once again, this time to the deep blue of a clear sky, or the hottest part of a flame. "Love."

Her mouth moved before she'd consciously thought the

words. "I agree."

"As stated, so shall it be." Lasair bowed his head, the magic of the binding surrounded them like a heavy blanket dropped on her shoulders.

As the binding settled over them, he raised his eyes. They'd returned to the orange and red hypnotic swirl. He licked his lips, and his fingers twitched.

Macari smiled. "I hope you find what you seek, Lasair." She held the cloth out and he took it carefully, like a lover would caress someone precious.

"*Your side of Agreement is complete.*" The words drifted past her ears, not spoken by either of them, but part of the binding that held them. The words died away as Lasair stared at the cloth so long she thought he'd forgotten her existence. The air around them felt pregnant with expectation. He had yet to fulfill his part.

And we applied no penalties to either one of us.

She hadn't spoken out loud, so it startled her when he answered. "I agreed. So shall it be. Take the Corsaerie, Walker. You seek Tarian Xannon, Keeper of the Water Artifact. Journey to the Edge, a place of power which will aid you in your task."

An image of a dimly lit room filled with dancing people and laughter filled her thoughts. For one instant, the detail seared her brain, like looking at the sun for too long, leaving an afterimage that faded slowly. Black and white tile floor, dark walls, lights overhead that glistened, tables lurking along the edge. She'd never, ever forget the way the room looked. She could use the scene to travel, once she stepped into the Wind again.

Lasair held out his hand, the rough black rock cradled in it. "Once there, open to the stone. Do not wait to bond, Naoise Sha'Macariah. Chaos is unpredictable, and not patient. Once the artifact has accepted you, and you it, use it to form a bridge through the Between."

She took the stone from him. Heat seared her fingers, burned up her hand and arm, into her chest. She gasped, and nearly dropped the stone into the grass, but managed to keep her fingers around it. It felt raw, untamed. Then the spasm passed, and the power diminished until she could no longer sense anything from the stone.

"Agreement is complete." Each had what they'd agreed to; she just hoped she hadn't taken on more than she bargained for.

Lasair returned his attention to the cloth. "Take the wind." He casually flipped one hand and Macari felt herself lifted. In seconds, she hovered above the trees, so high Lasair faded into the grass and disappeared. She hovered for a moment, astonished at the view. Trees, grass, and in the distance, ocean. And in the middle, fire flared.

The force holding her aloft vanished, and she plummeted toward the trees, wind pressing against her body. Holding the artifact in a tight fist, she closed her eyes and danced.

CHAPTER EIGHT

Macari stumbled out of the Corsaerie onto a cold, stone floor. Her knees buckled on impact and she collapsed, momentum rolling her into legs that ended in bizarre, pointy shoes. Her hand struck the shoe and ejected the stone, which bounced and rolled out of sight across the floor. With a squeal of frustration, she crawled after it, legs and feet parting for her as she moved.

The black and white tile floor swallowed shadows, turning everything dark. The black stone became a shadow, impossible to locate. As her eyes adjusted to the dim lighting of the space, her hands raked across the floor in front of her. It had to be here somewhere. It couldn't have gone far, there were too many obstacles. Feet, legs of chairs, a wall. It couldn't just disappear.

I hope.

She bumped into a pair of black shoes and snorted

impatience at the obstacle. Above, an amused voice asked "Looking for something?"

Macari glanced up. A handsome man with deep brown eyes and a pleasant smile held out one hand to her, offering assistance. He raised his other hand to show her the stone held between thumb and forefinger.

Heart pounding, Macari stood without help and reached to take it. "Yes. That."

The man held the stone aloft, just out of reach. He gazed at her with a curious expression. "If you tell me your name, you can have it. I like to know the name of every angel I meet." Desire pulsed over her skin.

"My name is Macari." She smiled as she ignored the blatant lust and snatched the stone from him. She closed it in her fist, heart pounding. Delayed fear roiled in her stomach and shoved into her brain. She could have lost it forever.

"Macari. I am so pleased to meet you." He licked his lips as if her name was a delectable morsel he'd love to eat.

She bowed her head slightly and turned away. *Bond with the stone* foremost on her mind, she pushed back onto the floor, to the center where she'd arrived. It felt like the center of power for this space, something Lasair had mentioned specifically.

The crowd that had parted in front of her now pressed in on her as they returned to what they'd been doing. Macari stood in the center, and watched as pairs or sometimes groups of three began gyrating to the beat of music she'd never heard before. Flashing lights overhead disoriented her, making her feel dizzy. Or maybe she was simply exhausted from crossing planes. Around her, people pressed against one another and lust poured into the atmosphere where it tickled her senses. Automatically, she took it in.

A man nearby smiled at her and winked as his gaze traveled her body. Macari glanced down, and saw her skirt hung in tatters that covered nothing, and her shirt lay in strips, which revealed most of the rest of her body.

Being naked didn't embarrass her, nor did the blatant attraction. Nothing could be more life affirming than a healthy exchange of energy. But she didn't have time for it. She needed to bond with the stone so it would remain hers. She opened her fist and studied the rock, frustrated by the dim light.

An uneven, hard, black husk shielded something bright gold and red, which poked through in small rivulets or veins. On one portion of gold she caught a glimpse of something dark etched there. She focused a bit of air and created a glow around the stone so she could see it better.

The heavy black lines disappeared under craggy black, not really decipherable as text. It could be a portion of symbol, but she couldn't see enough to confirm the idea.

How do I bond?

She thought about all Lasair had told her. His obsession with a fraction of cloth aside, he spoke in riddles like most Ancients. But she knew he spoke the truth. They all did. She'd never heard of an Ancient telling an outright lie. That was something humans and daemon did.

Since she could assume he spoke the truth, all she needed to do was decipher Lasair's meaning.

It will bond with one who is open, who fully accepts.

One who fully accepts what? How do I fully accept a lump of rock? Confused, she turned it over in her hand. The lines of gold and red reminded her of Lasair's eyes, fire waiting to burst forth through the crust.

When daemon entered into a life bond, they usually sealed it with an energy exchange that affirmed commitment, for the greater good. *I don't see how a stone can enter into an energy exchange.*

She turned it over, thinking. She couldn't manipulate earth other than to till soil with spears of Air. Breaking apart a solid crust of whatever mineral this was would be difficult, if not impossible. She couldn't work with fire except indirectly, the way any flame might need air in order to burn. Why would Lasair give it to her if bonding were impossible to accomplish?

The suspicion that perhaps he'd tricked her simply to get the piece of cloth Serin had tossed to her crossed her mind, but Macari dismissed it. His raw emotions had been pure. She'd detected no deception.

A slower song began to play, with a melody that enticed and encouraged physical movement and touch. Around her, Macari noticed the couples slow to barely moving, except for roaming hands and increased heart rates. Beats of power infused the song. Her body ignited in response to it, and she found herself swaying. Lights dimmed even further, with sparkles of white here and there turning the entire place into a magical fairy garden of lust.

The whole thing gave her an idea.

I should try an energy exchange with the core of the stone. It is, after all, pure fire energy. It needs Air. And that would make it a part of me.

She turned her attention back to the artifact and focused power. To do a full energy exchange, she had to open at least one of the carefully locked doors in her mind. Desire. It was the easiest to open, and the most fun. She eased the door open in her mind, letting the desire slip out. She funneled it down to the stone and focused on the red and gold swirls. Invited them to open, to bind with her power. Willed them to accept her, encouraging any display of power in return.

Enticing a response from another daemon this way had always been easy and entertaining. The stone, however, remained stubbornly silent, rejecting her advances as she'd never been rejected by a living thing. She pushed harder, letting more power and emotion through. It leeched through her skin, and into the surrounding air. As it struck people nearby, some hurried off the dance floor, while others began to take off clothes and fully engage in physical exchanges right where they stood. Moans, grunts, and general sounds of sexual encounters soon joined the music. She might not have noticed, except that a group of three nearby toppled into her in their rush to unclothe one another.

Startled, Macari gripped the stone and cut off the flow abruptly. Those already in the midst of lust would carry on until sated, but hopefully the rest would dissipate without much harm done. She watched the crowd, disappointment rolling through her stomach.

She pressed the stone against her chest, hoping the center of energy would yield some clue. In return, she felt nothing. The black rock lay cold and lifeless in her hand, a dead thing.

"You look like you could use a drink." A deep voice behind her made her spin in place.

The same man who'd picked up the stone stood there, his dark eyes sparkling in amusement. He held a glass out to her filled with something that smelled fruity. "I took you for a Sex on the Beach type of girl."

"I don't like beaches much." Bemused, she took the glass.

"Well, lucky for me we aren't on one. Shall we take this somewhere more private? Or would you rather dance?"

"I do like to dance." Macari smiled at him and handed him back the glass, hoping he would carry it, and himself, away.

"One moment, fair angel." He turned, and she walked in the other direction.

It seemed standing in the center of energy was a bad idea, since all it'd done was spread her power further than it normally would have gone. She needed power directed in a tight stream, not running rampant among humans. The place smelled of sex, which normally wouldn't be a bad thing. But sex bonding wasn't doing a thing to unlock the artifact.

I need a quiet corner to figure things out, to focus. Somewhere she could be unnoticed and, hopefully, shielded from errant overtures of power. Off to one side, a small alcove provided relief from the crowded dance floor. Happy to find an empty spot, she pushed her back to the wall and faded into the shadows. From here, she saw the entire room, but doubted anyone noticed her at all. Except for one man, who despite how much she'd dodged through the crowd, had followed with a determined look on his face.

"Angel, why are you hiding your light?" He held out a now empty hand in open invitation. "Dance with me."

"I dance alone." She frowned at him, perplexed and a little irritated. What was she supposed to do, touch him while she danced? It seemed odd.

"Alone is no way to go through life, precious. No harm in enjoying the company of another from time to time, wouldn't you agree?"

Something about this man made Macari want to keep her distance, though she couldn't explain why. She'd never felt that way about anyone. He seemed like a wolf, seeking prey. The glint in his eye matched his lust but not his words.

"You fascinate me. There's something raw and new about you. Something transcendent. I know it sounds corny," his cheeks reddened slightly. "I just have a feeling you're something special. Please. Take pity on a mere human and dance with me?"

He knows I'm daemon? As a small bit of fear raced through her veins, he took her arm, pulling her forcefully toward him with one hand while the other pressed into her back. She felt the sweat on his hands through the thin material, and smelled something sweet on his breath. Physical touch didn't happen often among the Benata. Such close contact let someone behind any shields one might have constructed. She pushed gently with one hand as she tried to step away from his arms.

He tightened his grip, keeping her pinned.

Anger flared, and she shoved the man backward both with her fists and a pulse of air. "I dance alone!"

He glared, took a step toward her. She readied her power, focusing a bit more than was probably necessary. Lust hit her full force, mixed with something close to greed. She let her talent take over and pulled both inside, locked them behind the doors in her mind, draining him at the same time. He stopped and stared, confused.

"Go." She said the word softly, but knew he heard as she gave it a little extra push of Air.

He waved a hand as though he wanted to argue, but then turned away, looking confused.

She watched him go, irritated, anger spilling out more than she'd usually allow. The stone cut into her hand.

"Well played." A soft, high-pitched voice next to her said in her ear.

Macari turned to see a woman, young, with long dark hair

and dark brown eyes, smiling at her.

"You should be careful. He gives bad vibes. He likes the blondes, so he never hits on me but I see him with other girls. Best stay away. I'm sure his dick is tiny anyway." The girl giggled and held out her hand. "I'm Anna."

Macari grinned. "I'm Macari." She stared at the girl's hand for a second, then extended her own. She'd seen it plenty of times, but it wasn't a normal way to greet someone on the daemon plane. Anna took her hand and shook it. Through the touch, Macari sensed compassion, pleasure, general happiness, curiosity. Nothing threatening, nothing lewd. *Air. Not much else.*

"Nice to meet you, Mac. If you don't mind me saying, you look a little beat up. That skirt's ready for the trash. You been in a fight or something?"

"Or something." Macari smiled.

"Well, you're obviously new here, so word to the wise. Avoid guys who drink first, talk later. And don't let the music get to you. They add a spell, so people get in the mood faster. It's to sell the back rooms and, of course, time with the hosts."

"Hosts?"

Anna pointed at her own chest. "I'm a host. We make sure all our guests have a good time. Except that guy." Anna raised her chin in the man's direction. He leaned against a wall, glaring at the room. "He don't pay, so he don't play. He's always trying to pick up a blonde for free. Sometimes he just sits and stares for hours. Real people watcher. Anyway, enough about him. You look like you could use a break. Come with me."

CHAPTER NINE

Anna led her through the crowd, off the dance floor, to the side of the room where an inconspicuous door broke up a long wall of artwork. Macari caught a glimpse of a mural depicting people in all sorts of naked poses and sexual acts, then she was dragged through the door and into a hallway. The door closed behind them, cutting off the sound of the music and the noise of the crowd.

As the sound faded away, Macari realized just how exhausted she was. So much emotion in that room, her talent had worked overtime to keep up with the flow. She felt drained, not just from that but from the trip and the attempt at unlocking the artifact. She needed rest, food, or an energy exchange. Or all three, if she was honest with herself.

Macari glanced down at the mark on her hand. Still visible, but faded from the dark black it had been at the beginning of her journey. Perhaps a quarter lighter. She rubbed it, wishing the blood rushing to the spot would darken it again. Completing her mission felt an eternity away. At this rate, she'd never finish before the mark disappeared completely.

Anna's open curiosity and concern forced a smile onto Macari's face. She must have been leaking. Fortifying mental shields she nodded. "I guess I *could* use a break. And a change of clothes." Macari looked down at the torn skirt.

"I got just the thing. There's a couch if you want some sleep, and a fridge with snacks. And there's bound to be something in the dressing room that'll fit you." Anna led the way down a long hallway, with doors on both sides. Sounds issued through the doors suggesting that those behind them were enjoying themselves in a private, physical way. Macari sensed various levels of energy exchange as they passed by them. *Strong enough to be daemon, but surely not.*

Baffled, she asked, "What is this place?"

Anna glanced at her over her shoulder. "This is The Edge. Didn't you know? How'd you get here?"

Macari hesitated. "I...followed directions." She couldn't explain, it would reveal that she wasn't human. Her mother had always warned her about how dangerous humans were for daemon. How the two should never interact. How humans were, at the core, basically evil. They didn't sense nature the same way, they didn't use magic the same way and they didn't see that society should come before all. Not to mention, it shouldn't even be possible for her to cross the planes to be here. "The barrier exists for the good of all, and should never be breached." Her mother's words haunted her, considering the same daemon had sent her to do the very thing she'd been taught to avoid.

Anna gave her a curious glance as they walked but didn't say anything. Macari wondered if the internal struggle showed on her face. She quickly checked her shields, and found them intact. Though she sensed a small amount of energy from Anna, she'd no idea where the girl's talents lay. Perhaps she sensed emotions too.

Anna pulled her through a door at the end of the hall, shutting it behind them. It cut off all sound and energy spikes from the rest of the club and provided a welcome relief.

Macari looked around as Anna crossed a room full of mirrors, tables, and racks of clothes. "First thing, let's get rid of those rags you're wearing. Go ahead and ditch them, I'll dig up something for you to wear. If you wanna shower, it's through that door to your right."

Macari shuddered at the thought of water covering her body. She knew that's how humans cleaned themselves, but she preferred a dry bath of air. Water made her skin itch. She felt it tingling now in anticipation. Instead of investigating the bathing room, she stood in the center of the larger space and watched Anna disappear behind a rack of clothes that took her breath away. *So many colors!* Nothing white, no white robes like court members wore, everything incredibly vibrant. Deep blues and greens. Vivid orange and yellow. She couldn't stop the surge of excitement and the hope that Anna would return with something so colorful it would give her mother a headache. She could almost hear her voice. "Daughter, dignity above all. You represent the Court at all times, in all ways." She rolled her eyes at the thought. *Why is white the color of dignity? Why can't other colors be dignified too?*

She ran her fingers over the nearest table and looked at the mirror surrounded by electric lights, the brushes and pots of color. Strange smells assaulted her nose, some earthy, some more like flowers. She focused on the lights. *No glow bulbs, no flame wicks.*

"Anna, why electric lights?"

"Because light bulbs run on electricity? Is this a trick question?" Anna's voice, muffled by the clothing, sounded confused.

Macari let her senses out to the room. Nothing in here functioned with magic power. Everything used technology, which didn't register on her senses at all. *How fun!* She grinned at it all. Science and technology, two things she knew next to nothing about. It exhilarated and fascinated her, begging for more interaction. She touched the bulb and yelped as she snatched her hand back to blow on the now burnt fingers. *They don't look like flames, but they sure feel like them.*

Anna emerged from the row of clothes with a dress in one hand and a skirt in the other. She held them up. "This dress would look amazing on you, but it's a bit flowy. Don't get caught in a gust of wind. The skirt will stay down, but it's kinda scratchy. You can wear almost any top with it, denim is good for matching. We can pick a blouse if you want. The dress will look amazing on you. Bring out your eyes."

Macari contemplated them. The skirt, straight and stiff, looked worn. The dress, a deep blue with swirls of green, reminded her of the view from the cliff. "That one."

Anna smiled and handed it to her. "Good choice. Go ahead, lose your rags."

Macari lay the dress down on the mirrored table, and carefully placed the artifact next to it. She pulled off what was left of her shirt, slid the skirt down past her hips, and had to admit the two together did look like a pile of discarded trash on the floor.

Anna sucked in a breath. "Damn, girl. You want a job? They'd hire you in a heartbeat."

Macari looked up at her. "Why?"

"Look at you. I mean, I could tell even with the rags you were wearing but still. You look amazing. You're like a doll. A really tall doll. And I have a feeling once you brush that hair you'll be movie star gorgeous. On second thought, maybe you shouldn't work here. The rest of us wouldn't look as good, next to you."

Macari glanced down at her naked body. It didn't look any different to her. "I look like everyone else. Breasts, feet. Everybody has them."

Anna shook her head. "Nah, girl. You got *it*. Embrace it. Own it." Anna continued to stare, her eyes softened as she took in every curve. Unlike some of the other inspections she'd experienced on the dance floor, Anna's admiration was direct, honest, and open. Macari smiled, to show she didn't mind the scrutiny. Something in the girl's gaze ignited a soft warmth and yearning within her own. She smiled again, this time letting that bit of desire into the air to play.

Anna took a hesitant step toward her, then two, until she stood within arm's reach. Macari inhaled deeply. The girl smelled like musk, a heady aroma that was earthy and feminine and so different from daemon that Macari lost herself in it for a moment, along with the emotions the girl sent out. She needed an energy exchange so badly, and Anna felt pure. She was full of interest, curiosity, desire…open, honest, and so full of life that Macari wanted to drink it in.

She touched Anna's arm softly, then brushed her fingers along her skin, pausing near the shoulder to make sure the girl didn't mind. When she saw the light in the girl's eyes, the interest, the trust, Macari put a hand on each of Anna's shoulders. She sent a tiny pulse of air, just a bit, just to test. Energy exchange involved wanting and accepting. Acceptance being the key component. She watched for signs. Anna's eyes widened as the energy flowed over her skin, then closed as she let it in. A soft sigh escaped her lips.

Macari ushered her own acceptance into the flow as she let her hands make their way slowly back down the girl's bare arms. Anna shifted and moaned, and then Macari felt a tiny answer of energy. She smiled, and whispered "Let it out. Join with me."

Anna opened her eyes, and shifted away slightly. She started to remove her blouse. Macari watched her, disappointed. "You don't want to exchange?"

Anna hesitated. "Of course I do. Isn't it obvious? I'm getting naked."

"Is that necessary?" Confused, Macari watched the girl strip until she stood bare. Breasts and nipples stood at attention. The heavy scent of her personal aroma strong and inviting. Soft thatch of black hair leading to her physical pleasure center. Legs, slightly open, an invitation. Passion and desire deepened to lust.

"How else we gonna have sex?" It was Anna's turn to be confused. "That's what you want, right? It's easier naked."

"Clothing doesn't matter. Here, let me show you. Stay still. Close your eyes."

Macari waited until Anna's eyes shut, then moved behind her. She blew air across the back of Anna's neck, shifting the hair. Her fingers traced a light path along Anna's arms, back and shoulders. She pressed close, not quite letting her breasts touch Anna's back, but close enough to reach around with her hands and lightly touch the top of the girl's breasts.

She exhaled along Anna's neckline, the breath soft, warm. Goosebumps jumped to attention along Anna's skin and the ridges of her nipples. Macari played her fingers over some of them as she pressed against the girl, letting bare breasts greet bare back. As their flesh melded, a shot of adrenaline and power pulsed.

Macari let her fingers drift lower, barely touching the skin, until they found nipples. Anna sucked in air, back slightly arched. She whispered into the girl's ear. "Join with me." Then closed her eyes and let magic escape. She cracked open the door in her mind which concealed desire. *Just a hint. A touch.* Enough to bring a moan from Anna's lips.   Macari let her hands drift lower, to Anna's power center, just below the heart. As she reached it, the girl moaned. Shifted feet that seemed suddenly unsteady. Then, after a long sigh, another tiny pulse of power reached the air.

"Let it out." Macari urged softly. "You're holding it in. Let it go."

Macari wrapped her own energy around the small amount she felt from Anna and urged it to grow. Teased it. Coaxed it higher. Eased off. Then *pushed.* Anna moaned.

"Shiiiiiit." Anna growled, her voice rough and raw.

Macari felt along the core of power. Tickled until it rang in her ears and made her teeth vibrate. Her body responded. Tensed with the pressure. Begged for release.

When her thighs heated and her core throbbed, Macari formed a ball of energy from their combined strength. It burst and, power poured over them. It felt like having a warm summer day reach out and give them a hug.

Macari's skin tingled as power settled like fine dust, giving back more than each had given. She absorbed the energy, drank it in like someone dying of thirst. Grateful for it, she threw her head back and teased a tiny bit more.

CHAPTER TEN

As their energy waned, Macari sighed, enjoying the surge, feeling replenished, strong, her body aches evaporated. The physical brutality of her walk on the Corsaerie whisked away by this tantalizing force so different from daemon. The sheer *life* wrapped up in the joining brought a giggle to her lips. Buoyed, she opened her eyes to find Anna collapsed on top of their discarded clothing. She'd been so involved in the exchange that she hadn't felt the absence of warm skin. But then, she wasn't used to having that particular addition to what usually amounted to a simple transaction. *It doesn't usually feel this intimate. This intense.*

"Anna!" Macari knelt beside the girl and felt her face. The girl's face was flushed and hot, as though she had a fever. *She's still breathing.* Macari tickled the girl's senses with a bit of Air. "I'm so sorry. This doesn't usually happen from a simple exchange."

Anna groaned and rolled onto her side. When she finally opened her eyes, she smiled. "Don't 'pologize girl. Shit. Best. Sex. Ever."

"Energy exchange, not sex. I'm sorry, I thought you'd know. I thought...I felt it, behind the doors. I thought everyone here knew." Macari helped the girl to her feet, steadying her while she caught her breath and regained her balance.

"Those doors. They...Mac, I don't know what you are...but you need to keep your head down. They figure out you're...just be careful. This place ain't always friendly. Just...get dressed."

Anna pulled on her own skirt with shaky hands. She shuddered.

"Damn, girl." Anna shook her head, eyes still dreamy from the exchange. "Energy exchange my ass. That was...I don't even know what that was. Shit." She rubbed her face with both hands.

Macari watched, uncertain. She couldn't sort out if the girl was pleased or upset. The girl's thoughts jumbled to the point that Macari couldn't read them. She frowned, alarmed with the possibility that she'd done harm, rather than good.

"I'm so sorry, Anna. I didn't mean..."

Anna shook her head, and smiled. "Told you, stop apologizing. Girl, I don't know what that was, but I'm gonna dream about it for the rest of my life. I feel..." Anna shook her head again. Closed her eyes and took several deep breaths.

Macari watched for signs that she would faint again, but the girl seemed steadier now. When Anna opened her eyes again, she looked more in control and exuded happiness. She pointed at the table behind Macari. "Put the dress on. If I keep looking at you like that, we might have to move in together. Never thought of myself as a lesbian but damn. Maybe I am."

Anna crossed over to a set of drawers on the side of the room. "Here, we have some clean undies. Not the most comfortable things, but they'll at least cover your privates." She threw a scrap of cloth to Macari, deep blue, satiny to the touch. "You don't need a bra. The dress will cover, and you're perky. Go ahead, put the dress on. I want to make sure it fits. Then we'll fix your hair."

Macari grinned. *I think she received more than I did out of that exchange.*

Feeling pleased, Macari took the dress and slid it on over her head. It drifted down past her hips as a cloud might drift through a valley. Then she took the undies and stepped into them. She'd seen under things in visions on the wind, but never worn any. She had to admit the feel of the silky fabric felt nice against her skin. The dress brushed against it, and the whole effect made her feel buoyant. She gave an experimental spin and the skirt flared up around her.

Anna laughed. "Yeah, it's a good thing you're wearing the underwear. You'll definitely get attention if you dance in that. Now sit, so I can brush your hair."

Macari glanced at herself in the mirror as she sat down. Her hair was matted in tight clumps of knots. Macari moved a section out of her face, seeing the Air mark on the back of her hand flash in the mirror. Had it faded a fraction since the last time she peeked at it? She rubbed it, noticing the tug of the bond as it tightened slightly. She'd stopped forward motion for too long.

"Nice ink. That tribal?" Anna leaned over Macari's shoulder to look at it. "Looks like it might need freshening up. Bet it'd look great on my thigh." Anna set to work getting the tangles out of Macari's hair.

Macari watched Anna in the mirror. Lasair said this place would help in her search. Perhaps the woman she sought was well known here. "Anna, do you know a woman named Tarian Xannon?"

Anna focused on a particularly difficult knot. "Sure. Everybody knows the Scion. Or *of* her. Keeper now actually."

Macari winced as Anna worked at the knots. She normally used air energy to untangle her hair. The brush was an instrument of torture. But if it kept Anna open to questions, she'd suffer through it. "Is she here?"

Anna laughed. "Girl, she wouldn't come to a place like this. We get some Sentinels from time to time. But this place...no Scion would ever come here."

"Do you know where she lives?"

Anna shrugged. "Near Hawaii. Why?"

It was Macari's turn to shrug. "I'd like to visit, that's all."

"I bet she won't be taking random visits from strangers right now, but you can try. Everybody has the right to petition for a meeting with the Keeper. You can use the alcoves, ask the Sentinels to get on her schedule."

"Why wouldn't she meet with me?"

Anna worked on a last stubborn knot with her fingernails.

"Well, I'm sure what with all that happened, they're being ultra-protective. Especially if the rumor's true."

"Rumor?"

"Got herself knocked up, didn't she? We heard the Succession Call for potentials even here. They won't want her at risk, not while she's pregnant. Bet they don't let her off that island until she gives birth." Anna brushed through Macari's now straightened hair. "I'm really jealous of your hair."

"Pregnancy isn't a weakness." Pregnancy and the surge of hormones always increased power in magic users. Someone as strong as Tarian Xannon would be a force to be reckoned with, while pregnant.

"Men. They get obsessed about things they don't understand." Anna arranged Macari's hair.

Macari closed her eyes for a moment, enjoying the feel of Anna's fingers in her hair. After an energy exchange, it was soothing and nurturing to feel someone teasing and combing and massaging. Now that her power felt renewed, she could focus on her goal of unlocking the artifact again.

The thought raced through her like lightning. *The stone!* Macari's eyes popped open and she searched the top of the dresser, frantic. *It's gone. It's not here.*

She jumped up, startling Anna who backed away, looking around. "What? You see a roach?"

"I...lost something." Macari shifted things around, hoping it was just hiding underneath a brush. When she didn't find it, she fell to her knees to search the floor.

"What? I'll help you look. An earring? What's it look like?" Anna joined her on the floor.

"It's a stone. A black stone, with gold and red."

They both patted at the floor, Anna crawled under the dresser to search behind it while Macari went the other direction in case it had been knocked off the top and flown a distance. Panic tightened her throat. *It isn't bonded. Anyone could use it. Anyone. I'll never complete my mission without it. Never get home.* The faded mark on her hand taunted her as she searched in vain for the artifact.

After several long moments, Anna stood. "You sure you brought it in here?"

Macari sat back on her heels, feeling defeated. "Positive."

A flash of something red caught her eye as she looked up at Anna. Something glinted out from Anna's black hair, something dark with flares of red and gold nestled there like a jewel. Macari stood slowly, her eyes transfixed on the artifact.

Anna froze. "I got something on me? I do, don't I. What? A spider?" She shifted anxiously. "I don't like bugs."

"Here, let me help." Macari moved close, leaned in, and plucked the stone out of Anna's hair. "There, gone."

She stared at the girl, feeling for any sign of deceit. Had she stolen the rock on purpose? Macari detected nothing but genuine concern, a bit of happiness, a dose of lust at their closeness. Macari smiled and kissed her cheek. "Thank you, Anna."

"For? We didn't find your stone."

"Just, thank you." Macari kept the stone tight in her fist and turned. "I should go. There's something I have to do."

CHAPTER ELEVEN

Anna led Macari from the room still looking a bit dazed. As they walked the hallway back to the main part of the club, Macari did her best to ignore the obvious energy exchanges happening behind closed doors along the hallway. The whole thing reminded her of the corridor inside her mind, each door enclosing a different emotion. This real-life imitation felt dangerous on a level she couldn't quite explain. She squeezed Anna's hand for comfort.

Anna nudged her with a shoulder. "Do me a favor? Come back some time? Next time, land in a corner instead of the middle. That's where most people pop in. Back by the booths it's less crowded, easier to make an entrance. I'll find you." The girl smiled, wistful. "At least, I hope I will. Word to the wise, don't drink anything. They boost it, to keep people here longer. It'll mess you up. In this place, it's best to keep a clear head."

Macari followed Anna out into the main room, instantly

assaulted by smells of lust, the thrum of music, and the incessant pull of magic. Anna squeezed her hand, then moved into the crowd and disappeared.

Macari wandered around the edge of the main room until she reached a long bar with stools supporting bodies of varying types and stages of undress. The energy level here really was astounding. She couldn't help but grin. Emotions ran rampant, with no attempts made to shield them. It was fun. There was nothing like it in Benata City, or anywhere on the daemon plane. *So much life here.*

A forceful hand on her arm spun her around. The man from earlier stood there, smiling, his eyes drinking her in. "Angel, when I saw you go out that door, I thought you had forsaken me. I can't tell you how happy I am you've come back. My soul longs for you. Say you'll take pity. Say you'll save me."

"You don't look like you need saving." She moved her arm out of his grasp, and tightened her grip on the stone.

"We all need saving. Everybody's looking for salvation of one sort or another. But only a few can find it, hopefully in the arms of an angel like you. Dance with me?" He nodded at the dance floor. "Just one dance. Come on, Macari, it won't kill you. It might even be *your* salvation."

"I have to go."

The man's eyes widened. "You can't leave, we've only just met! Please, you don't even know my name. It's Preacher, by the way. Everybody calls me Preacher. Have a drink with me then, if you won't dance? Just one drink."

Anna's warnings still fresh in her ears, Macari shook her head. "I didn't say I wouldn't dance. I said I wouldn't dance with *you*."

Anger flashed through his eyes and into the air. He pressed his lips together, then the cloud passed and he smiled. "You're too good for this place. A true angel. One that deserves special treatment."

"I have to leave." She tore her arm away and pushed into the crowd on the dance floor, ducking underneath and trying to mingle with the crowd. Anger from Preacher and his insistence followed her. She couldn't be sure if it was his, or her own. It surrounded her like a cloud.

Arguments broke out. Nearby, a glass shattered. The crowd, so lascivious mere seconds before, turned hostile. One man shoved another who fell into Macari, knocking her into a group of people. They caught her, then pushed back, shouting angry words she couldn't make out. The music rose to a fever pitch, a riot of sound that joined a kaleidoscope of colors. The doors in her mind jostled.

Macari covered her ears and ducked, trying to shut it all out. *Focus, Macari. Get control. Keep those doors closed.* In a panic, she pulled energy from the people around her, added it to her own and rushed to tighten every mental shield. The ones near the front settled down, but the ones further down the hallway in her mind were harder to contain, harder to seal. They threatened to overload. Determined, she slammed at the shields, tightened the locks. *Stars crash it all, stay closed!*

Heart pounding, she struggled with her internal battle and

lost track of everything around her. It took several long moments of internal swearing and deep breaths to calm her mind, restore stability, and stop the flow of anger. When she finally felt in control and satisfied the doors would remain closed, she opened her eyes.

Macari looked around, stunned. The crowd transfixed on her. They all seemed drained and confused. She'd not only locked away her own emotions, she'd locked theirs as well. Silence filled the room. Even the music had died away.

Nearby, Anna stared at her like she'd grown a new head. She could see the source of her anger and overload, Preacher, back by the bar. He stared as much as the others did, frozen. Macari closed her eyes and cursed. "Ciatch!"

I pushed too hard. Crash the universe and the stars within.

She stared at the source of her frustration and pondered what to do. The effect might wear off, or it might not. She'd never pushed a large group of people before, never let that sort of negativity out in full force. And it hadn't even *been* full force. *What would happen if I ever opened all the tightly closed doors to let the emotions run free?* She shuddered. *Nothing good can come of that.*

I have to give them something back. She'd taken the hostility and anger. The thing to do was open a door in her mind, just a bit, and let out something more positive to replace the stolen emotions. When she tried to jiggle a door open, it refused to budge.

Holding the stone so tightly it drew blood in the palm of her hand, Macari slowly turned. The only way to relax enough to let something out was dance. Dance always grounded her, helped her connect, allowed her join the Wind. While she wouldn't, or couldn't, take to the wind here, she could still dance.

She started to sway, pushed her body through the motions. Let her pulse slow. Her mind clear. She pirouetted, the new skirt billowing around her as if carried on a breeze. In her mind, she danced on her favorite hilltop, next to the Stulos, surrounded by Air, by the Shee, by her home. As she danced, she managed to open the door closest to the surface in her mind. Happiness. Just a fraction, enough to let it out into the room.

The music started back up, playing a lively song, breaking the spell. People blinked, confused, then turned to talk to one another. Several stole glances in her direction, but most moved on. Laughter punctuated the music, and the general mood lifted from nothing to joy in seconds.

She might have overdone it a bit. Guilt at having stolen and then giving too much ate at her. She tried to ignore it, but shame at having lost control settled on her shoulders.

Anna pushed through the crowd, gesturing. "Macari, wait." When the girl reached her, she was out of breath and excited. "I asked my friend, who has a cousin who used to be a Sentinel. Anyway, I have an idea where you might meet up with her," Anna lowered her voice. "Tarian."

Macari's pulse quickened. "Where?"

"She loves coffee. My friend's cousin's girlfriend works in Center City and sees her sometimes, at a coffee shop."

Macari tried to follow the information but it only confused her.

Anna glanced over her shoulder. "Preacher's heading your way. He looks pretty pissed. You should go."

Macari turned to see the man glaring at her, stumbling over chairs and people as he worked his way toward her. "I don't know where Center City is. I've never seen it."

"Here, follow me." Anna led the way to the corner, in the opposite direction of Preacher. When they reached it, Macari felt the girl weave power into a window, such as she used to view scenes while walking the wind. Confused, she studied it and the scene depicted within. A steady stream of people walked into and out of the scene. Lights flashed off to the right, and to the left, some sort of glass with drawings and writing painted on it. People sat at small tables, eating, while others flowed by non-stop. Macari saw a dark green bin filled with debris, and a small alcove with shiny metal pipes. It had just enough room for her to stand and not be in the stream of people.

"That's coffee?" Macari glanced at Anna.

Anna winked. "I'll distract Preacher." Anna turned and headed for the furious man advancing in their direction.

Macari paused, wondering if she should do something to help. Preacher watched her, but Anna put hands on his arms and Macari could tell she flirted. Playing the host. Entertaining her audience.

Macari turned back to the window, and once she had the scene firmly in mind, she closed her eyes to it, gathered power, and traveled.

CHAPTER TWELVE

Macari emerged on a busy street and quickly moved out of the way of people to push up against the wall of a building, a bit breathless. The transition had not been a smooth one and she'd nearly landed *on* someone. She took in a deep breath and coughed. The air smelled putrid, as though someone had died and the rotting corpse lay unattended. *Or urinated on. Yuck.*

To her right, several small tables and chairs filled a stone walkway. To the left, a dark opening led into an alley filled with large green bins full of refuse. In front of her, cars moved in both directions, making noise and filling the air with an even different sort of stench.

She'd seen cities on the Wind, many times. But the Corsaerie didn't transmit scents. Her stomach turned over once, then twice. Bile rose in her throat and she heaved once, bending over to clutch at her stomach with both hands.

Both empty hands.

Fear pushed her heart up out of her chest and into her throat. *The artifact! Where is it?*

It was in her hand when she traveled. She was sure of it. She had the marks on her palm to prove it. She looked around, frantic. *Did I drop it?* She cursed herself for not having locked it up, bound it to herself. Something. There hadn't been time. She'd been pre-occupied, first with exhaustion, then energy exchange, then with trying to bond with the thing. And then Preacher...

Anger bubbled up unbidden at the thought of *him*. She brushed it aside, impatient with her own lack of control. She had bigger things to worry about. *It was in my hand when I traveled. It has to be nearby.*

Stomach and stench both forgotten, she crouched low and started to search inch by inch. People tripped over her, but she ignored them and their rough irritation, her shields so tight that for once she didn't sense any emotions. She searched the nearby tables, the ground underneath them, the walkway, and the edge of the alley. She stopped when she encountered scruffy shoes and a body that didn't move out of her way.

The man leaned against the wall, watching her. His skin, darker than any she'd ever seen before, seemed to drink in the light. He wore a heavy brown coat though the day was warm. Tangled hair obscured his face. In one hand he held a package wrapped in brown paper with glass protruding from it, the other he used to prop himself against the wall. His head bobbed.

"You dropped out the sky. Gotta hurt."

"I didn't…have you seen a black rock?" Macari stepped into the alley. The shadows here were so deep, they'd obscure anything that small and dark. She could conjure up a light, but hesitated. The man next to her continued to watch. He had no magical talent at all that she could feel. Putting on a display like that seemed unwise.

"Lotsa black 'round here." The man grinned, displaying a mouthful of crooked teeth. "You like dark meat?"

"What?" She studied the area beneath his feet, behind him, and next to the green bin. Nothing. "Ciatch."

"Lady, you be careful back up in there. It don't be safe. Nothin' good come outta there." He waved the bottle at her. "You stay right here with Len. Have a drink."

"Um, no thank you." She shook her head.

The man furrowed his brow. "You need this." He stumbled toward her and pushed the package at her. "You dropped from the sky. You need this more 'n me."

Macari stared at him. Frustration welled up inside, tinged with fear and a fair bit of panic. "I need that stone. I can't go home without it."

"Home is here." The man stabbed his own chest. "Where you be, that's home."

"It's not…" she stopped. It wasted time, explaining something he wouldn't understand. Time that ticked away faster than she'd ever have anticipated. By the look of the mark on her hand, she'd lost a quarter of the time remaining. However time worked here, it was very different from the daemon plane. Faster. She swallowed, her mouth suddenly dry.

Len shuffled forward until he stood in front of her, swaying a bit as though caught in a strong wind. His eyes, deep brown, bore into her own. "Sometime, you gotta let it go. You wanna find somethin? Walk away. It'll show up when the time's right. Like this." He waved the bottle again. "Jus' when I needed it, bam. There it was. Like a good meal. When I needs one, it always there. You gotta have faith. Trust. Karma, she be a friend."

He took a deep swallow from the bottle. "Sometime she be a bitch. You gotta treat her right. Trust in her." He poked Macari's chest with an unsteady finger. "Trust in you. Let it go. If'n it meant to be, it'll be. Get me?"

Len shoved the bottle into Macari's hands. "Take it. You needs it more 'n me."

She watched the man shuffle off, weaving a bit, muttering something about angels. She studied the paper in her hands. Through one end, a glass bottle protruded, combined with a fruity smell that tickled her nose. She pushed the paper aside and found a dark bottle half full of liquid.

Let go.

Thirst. Fear. Panic. She had absolutely no idea what to do next. Where to even start looking. The artifact had already escaped her twice. Lasair warned her that it would be impatient to bond.

He really should have told me it would demand attention immediately. She put the bottle to her lips and sipped. The liquid tasted like cherries. It coated her mouth and tongue and burned its way down her throat. She wrinkled her nose at the bottle.

A pleasant warmth spread from her stomach and into her groin, out to her legs and arms. Whatever this bottle contained, it relaxed her body. She took another sip. This one didn't burn as much, though the happy warmth continued to spread. She grinned at it. It eased the thirst, and panic.

One more sip.

Her mission seemed all but impossible now. Time ticked away with the sun, and she'd lost the way to get home. Even if she found Tarian Xannon and gathered the information First Mother required, she couldn't make a report in time.

Where you be, that's home.

Macari studied the crowd racing by. It might be true. This might be her home, now. And it was foreign, confusing, filled with emotions and people and not nearly enough magic. It made her sad, how little magic she felt here. So very sad.

Macari stepped out into the walkway and joined the flow of people. So many people. She gathered their emotions like petals of a flower.

Next to her, a woman shouted into the air. *Anger. Frustration.*

In front, a man walked slowly, head down. *Pain.*

Across the street, a couple kissed. *Desire.*

Macari took it all in. So much emotion, more than anything

she'd felt in Benata City. Daemon always tried to lock away thoughts and feelings, to maintain privacy. It seemed humans didn't. Or couldn't. The doors in her mind jiggled. So many things to conceal and lock away. *Too many.*

The stronger emotions overpowered her defenses and popped their cages, racing out into the crowd around her like a raging bull.

Next to her, a woman screamed, and punched the man next to her. In the street, one car smashed into another and the noise filled the air with a sickening crunch and loud blast, following by shouts and thrown fists from people passing by.

Chaos erupted in the middle of the street. People streamed out of buildings, alleys, cars, and turned the immediate area into one big brawl.

Someone shoved Macari into the street, where she bumped into someone who in turn pushed her. She spun, directly into a fist. It connected with her cheek. Her face exploded and she ducked, cradling it in her arms.

Tears filled her eyes and spilled out.

Her defenses rattled, Macari struggled to get away from the madness. To catch her breath. To lock in her shields. The liquid she'd drunk made her slow, like she sloshed through deep water. The door which usually contained anger refused to close. Refused to lock. Helpless, she watched in horror as it filtered through the air.

While she couldn't see the actual power, she saw the effects and it devastated her. So many people, so very angry. Macari couldn't pull it back in, couldn't stop them from hurting one another. *And it's all my fault. I lost control.* And she never lost control. She'd practiced from infancy so that this very thing never, ever happened.

And here it was, everything she'd imagined it would be. *Disaster.*

Frantic, filled with the need to fix it somehow, she did the only thing she could think to do.

She opened another door.

The easiest to access, but also a good counter to anger. *Happiness.* She threw it wide and let it out, flowing like a river over the people. As it streamed, she twisted a blast of air energy into a weave of communication. It took her intention and magnified it a thousand times, so everyone touched by the emotion would know it was true, that it was theirs, that it was something to hold onto.

The crowd in the street erupted into laughter. Fights turned to hugs. Shouts to giggles. Frowns to smiles. Relieved, Macari let the flow drift away, her magic relaxed until the stream ended.

A man next to her leaned down and offered her a hand. She took it, getting back to unsteady feet. The man laughed. His eyes danced with pure joy, and though he didn't speak she smiled back, happy he no longer tried to punch anyone. He turned away to the next person and they laughed together, sharing a private joke.

Suddenly, she felt removed as though watching a party from a distance. Loneliness stole into her heart.

Laughter is the loneliest sound in the world if not shared. She took the unhappy thought and locked it away. Found an overturned chair, righted it, and sat down in the shadow of a building. Slowly the street returned to normal. People moved on. Traffic resumed. Life continued.

No sign of the artifact. No glint of red or flash of gold. No hope of finding it. *It's gone.*

She felt strained, shaken. The carefully concealed anger and happiness now loose in this world, the doors blown off their hinges. She couldn't lock them back in. It left her feeling uncertain, insecure, like something was missing. *Does this mean I won't ever feel happy or angry again?*

She tried to issue happiness again but it eluded her. Feeling an emotion on command required one in reserve. And now she had none. All she could muster was the very naturally occurring feeling of sadness and failure. Depression.

She couldn't afford to open any more doors, not here. The effects on humans appeared to be far more dramatic than they'd be on daemon, who maintained natural shields. She'd have to be more careful. No more strange liquid from strange bottles offered by strange men.

What do I do now?

Disheartened, she thought through her options. Continue to search for the stone in the hopes that it turned up out of the blue, as it had done in Anna's hair. Let it go as a lost cause, like Len the Bottle Man had suggested. If it was meant to be, it would come back to her.

Strange philosophy. But...perhaps with some merit given the fact that she had little alternative. She could continue her mission, in the hopes that this karma Len spoke of would somehow reunite her with the stone when she most needed it. Or she could give up. *Forget the mission, forget the artifact. Forge a new life here, on the human plane. Find a new home.*

She closed her eyes, imagining a life here, on this street. *No breeze. No hilltop. No home. No Stulos. No Shee. No First Mother.*

No Wind.

Macari gulped away the lump in her throat. No Wind. The thought stabbed at her heart, a physical jolt that made her eyes tear. To live a life here, in a place with next to no magic, and no access to the Corsaerie…

She rubbed at her eyes, then stared out at the street, not seeing it.

I don't belong here.

Almost as if he stood next to her, Lasair's words echoed back. *"No, you do not."*

You seek a woman named Tarian Xannon, Keeper of the Water Artifact.

Someone who held an artifact might be able to help her find her own. She also might know how to bond with one. At the very least, Macari could complete the task she'd been set. Get the information. Just in case she did find the artifact and was able to return home.

Time to find Tarian Xannon.

She thought of all she knew about Tarian Xannon. Between

the alley scene where Tarian had been attacked and the meadow, she could picture the woman quite clearly. Clear enough to reach her. *But that's dangerous. She could be somewhere else. And it didn't work out so well trying that in the Wind.*

Still. Her choice was either to wait here next to the alley until Tarian happened to show up, try to find Tarian at her home in Hawaii in the hopes they'd let her see the woman, or travel *to* Tarian directly and hope she remained stationary long enough to not cause problems in travel.

Macari looked around. The sun had dropped, casting long shadows. Fewer people filled the walkway, the other tables huddled deserted.

They keep her protected.

If what Anna told her was true, and The Keeper of the Water Artifact was with child, they surely would keep her isolated. She'd be unlikely to travel much.

Macari closed her eyes, and focused on the image of Tarian Xannon. Black hair. Blue eyes. Brown skin. She drank in every detail she could remember, down to the boots on the woman's feet and the mark on her arm from the attack. Everything.

When she had it center in mind, she gathered power, and traveled.

CHAPTER THIRTEEN

In the middle of what should have been instantaneous travel, Macari hit a solid wall of something that knocked her out of the conduit and out of breath. She plummeted from an unknown height, unable to provide a cushion of air before splashing into something warm and wet.

As her head slipped below the surface of water, shock gave way to panic and Macari fought against the enveloping embrace of wet. She'd gasped on impact, and received a mouth full of salt water that now burned her throat and lungs. Her head broke the surface briefly and she managed a cough and gulp of air before being sucked under by the waves.

She flailed against the sickening wetness. Beat at it. Pushed with her hands but it reformed over her head, pulling her down. Panic gave way to real fear, which used up any remaining air and thought in her head. She couldn't focus enough to use power of any sort, couldn't get her body to stop fighting, couldn't relax. Her battle against the tide lost before it ever began; she felt her body give up, her mind go dark. A hard bump against her backside did little except convince her life had ended.

I...hate...water.

Another harsh bump thrust her above the surface of the water. She convulsed and coughed, sucked under again only to be pushed forward. Around her, power surged, integrated with the hated wetness, enveloped her in comfort and a sense of peace that seemed out of place and completely inappropriate.

Macari let it take her body, and carry her forward. Warm air greeted and filled her lungs. Hands and feet found solid, rough ground. She crawled forward, coughing, buffeted by waves, until she'd crawled up onto a black sand beach. Her dress clung to her skin and formed a net that tangled her legs. Her skin felt covered in grime and wet.

She collapsed on the rough sand and panted. Tried to calm her mind from the near death experience. Lock away the fear. It refused to go, the trek down the long corridor of her mind too arduous. She let it flow out into the air instead. She didn't have the strength to argue with it, nor push her talent. It circled around her, a buzzard looking for fresh meat. Her heart pounded at it. Her mind swirled with it. The crash of waves nearby teased it. She encouraged the fear and then, as the waves receded, she pushed it out to sea.

When she felt more in control, and her breath no longer

came out in soggy hiccups, she sat up, taking a quick inventory of her surroundings. Black sand stretched in both directions, bordered by craggy rocks, lush foliage, flowers, and ocean along one side licking at the shore. No people, no living creature of any kind along the sand that she could see. She'd done something so foolish, so dangerous, that landing in the ocean was probably the least disastrous of the possible outcomes. *I could have died. I could have been trapped in the travel conduit forever. Dissolved to nothing.*

At least she'd managed to find her way out, but one thing was certain. Tarian Xannon was not here. Looking at the waves, she realized Tarian must be in the water, somewhere.

Macari sighed, disappointment creeping over her skin like the salt in the air. No way could she follow the woman into the ocean. She didn't even want to try. *Now what?*

Nothing for it but to wait. Surely she'd surface at some point. *But will she come back to this beach?*

A warm breeze stirred Macari's hair and tickled her senses. Though she'd find solace faster on a mountaintop surrounded by wind, she had to admit this place was relaxing and it felt nice to simply sit, letting the sun warm her. She ignored the ocean spray, focusing on the warmth on her face and shoulders and the breeze that worked to dry her hair and clothes.

Splashes offshore caught her attention, and she turned to see dolphins doing flips and playing in the waves. She smiled at them, and bowed her head, knowing this was what had pushed her out of harm's way. *Water Ancients.* She thought at them. *Honor to you.*

They giggled and clicked in response, sending a greeting to her thoughts. "*Welcome.*" An image followed the single word, of her in the ocean, playing in the waves. She thought back, "*Thank you. I can't swim. You saved me.*"

They splashed at her playfully, as if daring her to join them. She giggled and shook her head, scooting back as a wave threatened to cover her feet. She'd lost both shoes somewhere along the way, making it easy to dig her toes in the sand. Exhausted, she hugged knees to chest and rested her head on them.

Offshore, dolphins chattered another welcome message. Macari glanced up, smiling, then stopped as she saw a woman rising from the waves, one hand on a dolphin's back, the other pushing the water away to help her advance toward shore. Her dark hair streamed around her, water dripping off her body, which glinted in the sun. She wore very little, and her stomach protruded in obvious pregnancy. Around her, the Ancients flipped in the waves, a vanguard.

Tarian Xannon. Keeper of the Water Artifact.

Seeing the object of her mission alive and in front of her pushed Macari's pulse so that it raced along her veins. She forced herself to stay still and wait.

Tarian reached the shore and slowed her approach, leaving the dolphins behind her. She tugged at her hair, wringing the water out of it, looking at Macari as she made her way out of the waves and onto the sand. Confidence, and a sense of ownership, surrounded her. She didn't just arrive on the beach, she commanded it, and demanded attention, all without ever saying a word.

In person, Tarian looked even more like Serin than Macari had thought. Same darker skin, dark hair, striking blue eyes. The power emanating from her was infinitely more than anyone she had met so far on the human plane, and probably outstripped her own.

When Tarian finally cleared the water, she paused, still wringing out her hair, her eyes on Macari. Suspicion traveled on the air, but even if she hadn't felt it Macari would have known what the woman thought. Every muscle in her body was tense, though her expression remained calm. She didn't move closer, but Macari felt her weave some sort of power net. Not threatening, not active, more…seeking.

Macari remained seated, her toes in the sand, her body relaxed, her power dropped to inactive. She bolstered her mental shields, but otherwise waited passively, hoping the woman would read her non-threatening posture correctly. She didn't want to frighten anyone, and she sensed if this woman didn't like her, she'd make it known with force. Macari hadn't come here to battle. And Tarian looked like she could break Macari's body in half without the use of magic, even while pregnant.

Macari grinned at Tarian, exuding friendship and happiness, and waited, her toes curled, her fingers playing in the sand. She peeked at the mark on her hand. It seemed even lighter. *Seeing her isn't enough. Knowing she's pregnant isn't enough.* She thought quickly. *What else am I supposed to learn? Why Tarian joined with*

Ruarc. How am I supposed to get that information from a stranger?

Tarian blinked, finally dropped her hands and walked toward Macari. She remained in a state of alertness, evident from the tension in her arms to the way she planted her bare feet on the sand. She kept her face neutral, and only one emotion preceded her across the beach. *Determination.*

She stopped a few feet away from Macari, feet shoulder width apart, arms by her sides but tense. Ready for a fight.

Macari kept her hands down, her focus to a minimum. "Well met." She kept her tone light and friendly.

Tarian lowered her head slightly. A nod. Acknowledgement. Suspicion clouded her eyes. "Hey." She watched Macari draw in the sand for a few seconds before adding. "Who are you?"

"Macari." She squinted up at the woman.

"Tarian." The word was almost a grunt.

"Well met, Tarian."

Clicks and giggles offshore made them both turn their head, though Macari suspected for different reasons. The dolphins sent no more thoughts her way. All the same, she saw something glinting near one of them. As she watched, it flicked its nose and something shiny rose high in the air, traveling directly toward her, like someone tossing a ball. A very dark, small ball.

A ball that wasn't a ball. A dark shape with glints of gold and red that as it drew closer resolved itself into...a rock.

It landed on the beach with a thump, half-buried in the sand. Macari stared at it, her mouth hanging open in disbelief.

The artifact.

Tarian picked up the stone just as an ocean wave washed over the area. She squinted at it, bringing the rock closer to her face. She closed her eyes, and Macari could feel the focus of power directed toward the lump of black. *She's testing it, to see if it's dangerous.*

When Tarian turned around, her eyes flashed annoyance. "This yours?"

CHAPTER FOURTEEN

Macari sighed at the rock. "Not really."

"You sure about that?" Tarian tossed it to her, and Macari scrambled to catch it. It fit neatly in the palm of her hand as though it belonged there. *Sure doesn't seem to like me very much.*

Macari frowned at it. "Unfortunately."

"My friends tell me I shouldn't pick a fight with you. They assure me you're no threat. Is that true?" Tarian crossed her arms over her belly and glared at Macari as though she'd just stolen something.

Macari grinned up at her. "I'm a dancer, not a fighter."

"You're a lot more than that." She lowered herself awkwardly to the ground, letting her belly protrude out in front of her as she leaned back on her hands. The sun had already dried most of her body but her hair was still wet and tangled by her swim. "What're you doing here, Macari?"

"You're not going to hit me?"

Tarian's lips twitched. "You want me to?"

"No." Macari hesitated. "But you obviously don't trust me."

"Would you?"

"Yes. Though, perhaps, that might not be wise." Macari glanced out to sea, where the dolphins kept watch, strangely silent now. "You have interesting friends."

"So do you." Tarian pointed at the stone. "Powerful ones."

"I wouldn't call him a friend. I only met him once." Macari shrugged. "I'll probably never see him again."

"And yet he gave you an artifact of power. The Fire Artifact, to be specific. Why is that?"

"I was convenient." She grimaced. "Even if he did give it to me, it's no good. It's not working and every time I…" She let her voice drift away. Maybe telling the entire story was a wrong move, at this point. She needed this woman's help and wanted her friendship. Something about her made Macari want to protect her. She felt loyal to this woman she'd barely met, for no good reason at all.

Tarian turned her face to the sky as though she were a plant absorbing life energy. "You're daemon." Her words were flat, not an accusation, merely a statement of fact. "How on earth did you get here? Do you have human blood in your family?"

Macari laughed. "Of course not."

"I thought only someone with both daemon and human blood could cross the Between."

"Apparently not." Macari paused, wondering if it were true. And if it were, exactly what that meant. "Though I suppose I had help."

"Fire Ancients?"

"And the Wind."

"Fire and Air?" Tarian lowered her gaze. "Interesting combination."

A cloud passed over the sun, dimming the landscape.

Hoping to move the conversation closer to the information she sought, Macari offered a bit of background. "I fell out of the Wind in the right spot. A meadow, on the edge of the Between. That's where he found me." She waited to see if Tarian recognized the reference, but the woman gave no sign that she noticed anything.

"Why'd you come here, Macari? Or, more importantly, how?"

"I told you, I…"

"Fell out of the Wind into a meadow. That's not what I mean." Tarian narrowed her eyes. "Why are you here, on my beach?"

Macari hesitated. Never before had she been faced with such an important decision. *Tell the truth, about my mission, or lie? What's the right move?* Would the woman respond to the truth with friendship and information? *Unlikely.* She'd probably feel threatened, at the very least. But if she detected a lie, they'd never establish any sort of trust. Either way, the mission wasn't likely to be completed.

"The answer's that complicated, huh?"

"Incredibly." Macari stared out at the ocean where dolphins remained, watching. She clutched the fire artifact, letting it dig into her palm again. "I can't go home. I have to unlock this artifact to catch the Corsaerie from here, and it's not responding to anything I try. I was hoping you could help."

Tarian rubbed her belly, obviously thinking. A flash of emotion followed the movement, so raw that Macari blinked as it washed over her. *Worry. What in the stars could make this woman, so powerful and obviously competent, worry?* The only answer was the baby. *She's worried about being a mother.*

"Pregnancy makes you stronger, not weaker, you know." Even now, Macari could sense the baby. Not as fully formed thoughts or intentions, but the power in that one tiny person was unmistakable. She pulled from everyone around her, though they didn't seem to be aware of it. She pulled on Macari's own energy, not enough to drain her but enough to notice. "How long?"

Tarian glanced up, startled, her eyes wide. "Five months. Give or take. I still have four to go."

Macari frowned. The child felt older than that. Much older. By the feel of her, Macari estimated Tarian had two weeks, perhaps three at the most, before the child joined the world. If she were this strong now, what might she be when she reached her naming day? The thought sent shudders down her spine. *Amazing.*

Tarian held out her hand. "Let me see it again." She examined it from every angle, then held it in her palm, eyes closed. A thrum of power flooded the area. "Your signature is all over this thing. How did it end up on my beach *after* you arrived?"

"I lost it in travel."

"And it followed you here?" Tarian kept her eyes closed. Macari watched her work, fascinated. The energy she used, a complicated weave of air and water, hummed with power. Yet the stone didn't react at all, either to the probe or the woman herself. It didn't try to bond with her as far as Macari could tell.

"I don't know. I searched but didn't find it. I didn't think I'd see it again, so I followed the man's advice and…" She'd been about to say "gave up to find you instead." But that would lead back to her original mission.

Tarian opened her eyes and looked out to the ocean. "The dolphins told me you're hiding from something. Or someone. Or it might have been that something is hiding from you, it was hard to tell. What're you hiding from, Macari?"

"I…" Macari pressed her lips together, struggling with what to say. How to complete her mission and not alienate the woman at the same time. "Fire doesn't like Water."

"Oh, I think sometimes it does." Tarian waited.

Macari glanced at the ocean, where the dolphins had formed a circle and floated there, watching them.

The waves rushed the shore, then slowly withdrew, only to rush once more. *What I wouldn't give for a good blast of mountain wind right now. Something to make me feel solid and in control again.* Since she'd opened the door to anger and happiness, she'd felt unbalanced and out of sorts. Nearly drowning hadn't helped.

Macari glanced at her hand. Time ticked away with the ocean waves. *I have nothing left to lose really. Why not be honest? I came here for help, after all.* She took a deep breath, then squared her shoulders and sat up a bit straighter. Looked down at the sand, absorbing the way it sparkled in the sun. When she spoke, her voice sounded soft and vulnerable. But she pushed on. "I see things, on the Wind. Scenes from past events. I saw you attacked by the Laghairtine. The blood. The way you fought with water, and he with fire. I saw you in that meadow, with the leader of the Mayfanata."

She glanced up to see how Tarian took the news. Tarian's face remained calm. Encouraged, Macari continued.

"I was sent to find you. To find out if the joining was successful, and to find out why you did it. Or, I suppose, why *he* did it. I'm a Wind Walker. I'm the only one who can travel on the Wind wherever it goes. So I traveled to the meadow, but instead of finding you I found Lasair. And he sent me forward. But from here, I can't take the Wind, so I'm trapped. Unless I bond with the artifact." The words came out in a rush. Now that she'd decided to tell the story, she wanted it out as fast as possible. "That's why I'm here."

Tarian nodded, her chin jutting out in an expression of contemplation. She glanced over at the rocks, shook her head, then back at Macari. Macari followed her gaze but saw nothing. When she looked back, Tarian rubbed her belly with one hand. "Well I suppose you answered one of those questions at least."

It was Macari's turn to nod.

"Wind Walker." Tarian savored the word, drawing it out. "This is the first time you've come to the human side?"

"It's not easy. Usually I stick to the outer edges of the Corsaerie, but I went deeper…and saw…well, that part doesn't matter. Mother certainly didn't think it did. She's much more worried that Ruarc does nothing that doesn't benefit himself, and she worries what he gained by…"

Tarian grunted, and rubbed her belly again. "I've wondered the same thing. She's right to worry about it. I got the feeling he had an agenda, but at the time, it didn't matter." Tarian paused, head tilted as she considered something. "Are there others who can walk the wind?"

"Not of the daemon. Not that I've ever heard, anyway. To Walk takes special talent. You have to let go of self and merge with the stream."

"Go with the flow?" Tarian's lips twitched.

"Yes." Why that should be funny, Macari had no idea. "It moves fast, and control is impossible. Most daemon don't enjoy letting go of control."

"Hmmm". Tarian sat up straighter and studied the artifact once more. Tarian closed her eyes. Macari remained silent, feeling the thrum of power exchanged from rock to woman and back again, in time to the stroke of the ocean waves. When Tarian opened her eyes, they lit up with curiosity and something else. Fascination?

Tarian handed the stone back. "Why haven't you bonded with it?"

"I don't know how." Macari took it, wrapped it in a fist.

Hard, unfeeling thing just lay there unresponsive.

"You sure about that? You've already cracked it a bit. See, on the side?"

Tarian leaned forward to point at a ridge Macari hadn't noticed before. More of the symbol showed through a missing chunk of black. "Oh." What had happened to cause it to crack and break? How could she repeat it?

"You know how. You said it yourself, you have to let go to join the stream. Maybe you have to do the same to join with the artifact. I know for me that was true. So it seems the Ancients are right. You *are* hiding from something. Yourself." Tarian smiled, softening the words. She muttered "Ironic." So softly Macari almost didn't hear it.

Tarian seemed like the type of woman Macari could be friends with. Someone she'd like to know. She smiled back, letting gratitude color the air.

Footsteps crunching on the sand alerted both of them to the approach of a very tall, muscled, dark brown skinned man dressed in white. He ushered frustration, concern, and worry ahead of him like a flock of birds that scattered as he stormed through them.

"Before you get all up in it, just relax. It's fine." Tarian struggled to her feet, her pregnant belly making the maneuver awkward. The man joined her and stared down at Macari as though assessing which part of her he'd like to dismantle first. "Alex, this is Macari. The dolphins rescued her from the ocean."

Alex frowned down at her. Macari shielded her eyes from the

sun and smiled at him, exuding a bit of friendly polite happiness. "Well met." Her tone turned up at the end like it was a question, not a wish for good humor. Alex's mouth twitched.

Tarian held her hand out to Macari, offering to help her up. "If Lasair gave the stone to you, then you are the one he means to bond to it. I only smell two signatures on it. His, and yours. Wherever it ran off to, it hasn't been claimed. Yet. You should try again. Just do me a favor and don't unlock it here. I'm not sure how the Dolphin Throne would react."

Tarian ran her fingers through her hair, working out tangles. "You might also think about why this artifact was given to you, in particular."

"I was convenient." Macari took the extended hand, half-afraid that if she didn't, Alex would haul her up and forcibly dunk her back in the ocean. "And I had something he wanted."

"I'm sure it's more than that. Ancients aren't that simple in their motivations. Kinda like daemon that way." Tarian smiled at her, eyes crinkling at the corners. "He had a reason for giving it to you, or at least, a reason to *let* you bond with it. A reason to think you *could*. Think about what your talents are, and who *you* are."

Macari caressed the rock. "I read emotions. That won't help. Can't get feelings from a stone."

Tarian raised an eyebrow and shared a look with Alex that Macari couldn't interpret. The only emotion conveyed was interest, curiosity. Not a lot of help. Something about her ability interested Tarian but then again why wouldn't it?

"You sure?" Tarian smiled, a gentle warmth on her face that lit up her eyes. "I bet if you try you'd get something from this particular stone. After all, it was crafted by Ancients. The Dolphin Throne uses images and emotions to communicate, among other things. Not sure this one would be any different. Besides. You're more than just one talent. Right now this stone is just a spark. You have to build it to a flame. All it needs is…"

"Air." Macari grinned. "Fire needs Air in order to burn."

Tarian nodded. "It does." Tarian extended a hand to Macari. Macari took it, and through the brief touch felt Tarian's power, stronger than her own, hovering, along with confidence and a whole host of emotions that didn't show on the woman's face at all. Macari quickly probed a bit further, and felt another, different stab of power. Something within Tarian pulled at Macari's intrusive energy and played with it. Happiness, joy followed along and tangled everything up, pulled it in, then let it out expanded several times over the original signal. Macari gasped and pulled back.

Tarian looked at her questioningly but didn't reach out again, seemingly oblivious to the exchange. "Good luck, Mac. I'm here if you need me. Just, next time use the travel alcoves." Tarian pointed to a large craggy opening in the rocks ahead. "Landing on the beach might get you shot."

Macari nodded and watched Tarian waddle up to the opening and through, disappearing from sight. *That baby is awe-inspiring. She doesn't know what she has. A child like that could rule the world. Or destroy it.*

CHAPTER FIFTEEN

Macari watched Tarian disappear into the dark opening in the rocks, lost in thought.

Think about your talents. You hide from yourself. Let go.

Fire needs Air in order to burn.

Off to her right, Alex cleared his throat and she glanced up. Broad shoulders, dark hair, deep pools for eyes, slabs of granite for hands and deep brown skin. He was the most beautiful male she'd ever seen.

He radiated curiosity, caution, loyalty, and impatience.

"Why'd you land in the ocean?" His voice, deep and with a heavy lilted accent that made her smile.

"I didn't mean to. I tried to travel to Tarian directly, but then hit a wall or something." She rubbed her shoulder at the memory. It'd hurt, but then she'd nearly drowned and forgot about it.

"Score one for defense." Alex grunted. "But minus one

for swimming."

"I don't understand."

"You hit a shield. We shield everything but the travel alcove. But we can't shield the water. Too big."

"But I can be here now?"

"Yeah, that's giving Frankie fits. No offense, but you shouldn't be here."

Macari felt the air for any shield. She felt nothing. "That can't be why I dropped out of travel. I don't feel a shield. Whatever you used, it doesn't work on daemon."

Alex stared. "Good to know."

"You don't trust me."

"Don't know you." Alex crossed his arms, and leaned against a large rock.

Trust. Something that in Benata City was assumed, expected, and forgotten. With so many open minds, it was easy to forget that some could keep secrets. Humans, especially. They didn't connect mentally as daemon did, so hiding truth had to be easier.

But emotions don't lie. Right now, Alex didn't feel hostile or devious. Just cautious against her intrusion. Wary of a possible threat. She had no intention of harming anyone, but he couldn't know that. Not unless he joined her in mind-speech. Somehow, she didn't think that would be welcome. Or even possible. He didn't feel like Air. He felt heavier. Grounded. *Earth maybe.*

"I guess I should go now." She hesitated, the stone gripped in her palm. Where was she supposed to go? She only knew three places. The crowded city, full of humans with no magic, where she'd wreaked havoc with one emotional outburst. The Edge, full of magical ones, where she'd wreaked havoc, again with one emotional outburst. This beach, which she'd been specifically warned against.

She definitely couldn't use the beach, not with so many powerful humans nearby, including one very pregnant, very important one. The street lacked any magic to help bolster if she needed it. That left the Edge. A place of power. Surely they'd forgotten the earlier event by now. They'd have moved on to more dancing and joinings. She could find a dark corner, and, as Tarian said, let go. With all the extra magic in the air and everyone focused on their own energy release, they probably wouldn't even notice her.

Right. She knew they would. But this time, she'd establish a shield first. Or something. Instead of letting emotional energy run rampant, she'd channel Air. Pure air.

"Want me to have a look?" Alex pointed at the artifact. "I'm good with rocks."

"It's not a rock, exactly. Though I suppose it looks like one."

"Lemme see." Alex held out a hand, and Macari gave him the artifact and watched it disappear into his palm. He closed his fist, took a deep breath, let it out slowly, then took another. Held it. Let it out. He did this a few times while she admired the bulge of his arm muscles and the way his chest rippled with effort. She could feel him concentrating and focusing, his power rippling along with his muscles. He was strong, but not as strong as Tarian. *Or the baby.*

Alex grunted and handed the stone back to her. She took it, liking the warmth it had generated in his hands and the touch of his fingers on hers. She shivered, feeling a surge of energy that wanted to join with his. *Now wouldn't that be an exchange!* Feeling the answering surge of lust, she grinned at him. His eyes sparked from interest, but he didn't mention the small exchange.

"It feels like lava, turned to stone. Pressure and time makes a rock like that. Pressure's the only thing that'll release it."

"What sort of pressure?" She let her senses drift over the artifact again.

"Heat, maybe. It's contained and needs release. Sorta like a thunderstorm. Just needs a bit of heat to break open, let the rain out." Alex ran a hand through his hair. "I'm not making sense."

Fire needs Air in order to burn. "Actually, you are. Thank you, Alex." She clutched the stone in her fist and smiled up at him. "That helps."

Alex shrugged.

They waited, each one trying not to stare at the other. The air was pregnant with expectation, though what it waited for she hadn't the slightest. Finally she realized. *He's here to watch and make sure I leave.*

"I'm going."

"No, wait." Alex held out a hand as if to stop her, then ran his fingers through his hair instead. "You need help? I could go with.

Help you work it out."

She smiled. "You don't trust me, but you'd help me anyway?"

"I trust you." Alex protested.

"No, you don't. You shouldn't. You don't know me, Alex."

Alex narrowed his eyes at her. "Tari trusts you. Is she wrong?"

"She has good judgment?"

His lips formed a lopsided grin. "Sometimes."

Macari stepped closer. "Thank you, Alex. But I think this part of the journey is mine to take. If I can't sort it out, may I return?"

"You heard the Keeper. Anytime." Alex stared into her eyes and for a moment they held a connection as old as time itself. Something about him tugged at the core of her heart. Like she'd known him a thousand years. *Maybe I've seen him on the Wind.*

She inched closer and tilted her face up to his. He looked down, his eyes half closed. *Desire. Confusion.*

Macari pressed her lips gently to his. It was a swift movement. An expression of gratitude. Through the touch, she sensed loyalty, passion and love for someone. His yearning for something he couldn't have. It was so similar to what she'd felt from Lasair that she did a double take. *He's in love with someone he can't have.*

"Thanks again. To both of you."

"*No problemo.*" He whispered.

She squeezed his hand, and sent a short pulse of energy to him. Just a small bit of magic, given freely, to bolster his own. It was her way of flirting, and she knew he'd received it that way when his cheeks reddened and his grip tightened. He shifted from one foot to the other, and cleared his throat. But he didn't release her hand. *A good sign.*

"Well met, Alex." Macari let the tiniest amount of trust, loyalty and friendship color the air. Those doors, close to the surface, were easy to open. While he didn't echo the sentiment, he'd stopped sending *dis*trust, and that was a start.

Alex released her hand and stepped back. "The alcoves are this way."

"I don't need them." She smiled, focused, and traveled.

CHAPTER SIXTEEN

Macari emerged in the darkened corner next to the booths at The Edge.

Music in the club raced over her body. The beat exactly matched her heart, the rhythm in tune with her own. She let it revolve as she examined the room. The energy level had elevated since her abrupt departure. More people, more magic, a lot of raucous laughter, and body exchanges happening all over the place filled the air with power and possibility. If she harnessed it all, she could try to use it to apply pressure to the artifact. Perhaps it would help her let go and truly bond. It was worth a try, especially since she didn't really have any other ideas.

She squeezed the artifact tightly in her fist and joined the crowd in the center of the room where the power levels were strongest. She could tap into it and weave it with her own, joining the stream as Tarian had suggested. This time, instead of siphoning all emotion from the room or sending everyone into happiness overload, she'd direct pure Air toward the artifact.

Macari focused power and let it roam to join the energy in the room. Music and people combined to create a mix of sounds that stimulated her senses. Her body swayed, everything in her wanted to dance and join with the exchanged energy. She resisted the urge, and instead opened herself to it while her feet remained rooted to the spot. Energy surged. She funneled the stream to the artifact.

As magic channeled through her, she used it to form a beam of pure Air, which she shaped into a net surrounding the stone. Her hands heated from the effort, and a trail of warmth traveled up her arms and into her body.

Macari buried her senses into the artifact. The shielding remained intact, stubbornly refusing to even crack. *More pressure. Like a storm.*

She tried the reverse of what she'd been doing, and created instead a vacuum within the net around the artifact. The pressure made her ears pop. A scream erupted somewhere, a primal sound that filled the room as her energy dispersed it through the atmosphere along with her frustration, disappointment and something more. Rage. It took her by surprise. It shouldn't have been so easy to tap. But now, suddenly, it rushed the door as though it didn't exist and launched through her, a bolt of jagged, searing, violence. She staggered as it plowed through her mind and out into the surrounding atmosphere unfettered.

The room erupted in shouts, screams, and jostling bodies.

Her concentration and focus broke, and like a dam suddenly releasing all the pent up force of water, power poured from her hands and into the room, along with a jolt of Fire that bathed them all in heat. It circulated through the room, causing chaos and fires to erupt on all sides.

Macari shuddered, her body in spasms, hand so tight on the stone that she couldn't tell where one ended and the other began. She tried to dampen the outpouring of energy but it was too late. So much poured into the crowd that they responded in kind, adding theirs to hers in a whirlwind of power, sound, fury.

Throat constricted, sweat pouring down her face, shaking, she did something she'd never done before and cut the flow of power she supplied completely, abruptly. Like slamming a mental shield in place, but this time she pushed it around her until she cut herself and the stone off from the rest of the room.

The artifact glowed in her hand. Heat radiated from it as though she'd plucked it straight from a fire. But the treasure below remained hidden from view. She'd failed.

Furious, frightened people all turned toward her. Fires raged everywhere, though even as she looked, they died down to mere sparks, their fuel gone. She saw Anna on the edge of the room, screaming, gesturing wildly, pointing madly at something behind her, but couldn't make out what the girl was saying. The shield she'd created dampened sound. The crowd surged forward, toward her. The only clear message she could make out was "get out." But her shield stopped them, and Anna, from coming any closer.

Macari turned and ran, pushing Air in front of her to cause a break in the crowd. Desperately she tried to focus enough to travel, but her body was spent. She couldn't do it.

Ahead, wavering air formed a bubble she could just make out through the press of people. As she pushed toward it she saw it was a window, like Anna had created earlier. *Bless her.*

She raced for it. *I can do this. Just breathe, Macari. Focus. It'll calm down here after I leave. I hope.*

Focused on the window, Macari stumbled over something in the floor and fell, landing awkwardly on her knees, hands automatically thrust out to catch her fall. The stone shot out when it hit the floor, skittering across it in front of her, rolling away as it'd done before. She growled in frustration and thrust a curtain of air toward it.

"Run!" A voice, high pitched and familiar, urged her forward. The sound, loud in her ears, told her the protective shielding had vanished when she'd dropped the stone. She was simply too distracted to keep it all going.

The artifact hovered in front of her, momentum slowed by the air net she'd thrown. She stumbled to her feet and at the same time pulled on the net, dragging the stone toward her body even as she moved forward. Her pulse raced as though it had somewhere else it needed to get to, in a hurry. Lights flashed overhead, a dizzying mix of lights and darks.

Her desperate moves through the crowd had brought her close to where the shimmering window hovered. The scene, a room with dark brown walls, blue columns, wavy undulating light, and a black/white tile floor.

Behind her, a shout. "Look out!"

A shove, and Macari stumbled forward and fell toward the window. With a last desperate pull, she tugged on the net, dragging the stone with her as she plunged through the window.

Cold. Intense cold, and her body dissolved into nothingness that was wide, white, expansive, eternal.

CHAPTER SEVENTEEN

In the vast expanse of nothingness, Macari tried to get a sense of direction or even a sense of up and down, but found nothing. Her body didn't exist, so how could she find up and down? Left or right, top or bottom, all gone. Hands, gone. Feet, gone. Her mind floated in a sea of white. And cold. So cold she'd have shivered if she had a body.

What is this? What happened? Did I die?

Cold ate at her. It dissolved her fortitude and stole her breath. Her thoughts scattered, unable to even form the intention to focus power. All around her she felt energy above and beyond anything she'd ever experienced. But it didn't act on her. It didn't do anything in particular; it simply existed.

Overload. I'm going to overload.

If she had a mouth, she was sure it would be bone dry. If she had a pulse, it would have throbbed so hard in her throat that it might have escaped.

Oh stars and Wind, I'm…nothing.

In the midst of the nothing, a soft sound emerged. So faint. Then it grew louder, as a whisper spoken soft against an ear that didn't exist. The brush of a soft breeze on a leaf.

Those who play with fire are bound to get burned. A giggle followed, sounding almost maniacal in this situation.

Unable to speak since she had no body and no mouth to use, Macari opened her mind to communicate. *Jasmine?*

Wind Walker, revolving in air, a destination before you, reach for it; it's there.

I don't know the destination. I…don't know where to go. Why can't I travel?

Walker of Wind, taker of time, you're already traveling, a journey in mind.

Another whisper began on top of the first. *Remember the scene, have it firmly in mind, I promise you, you will reach another side.*

Desperate, Macari searched her own power. But every time she pulled on it, it seemed to join the chaos around her. How could she reach for something with no power?

Little Wind Walker, holding the flame. Fire needs Air. It's yours to claim.

She'd never fallen into a window before. They were for viewing, nothing more than a glimpse of the past. All this talk of fire wasn't helping in the slightest.

Cold. Bitter, never ending, relentless, cold.

Window. Could it be the window she'd seen was more than just a way to view a distant place? Could they, on this plane, be used for traveling?

Macari thought desperately of the scene she'd witnessed through the window. Tried to pull her incoherent thoughts together to form intention. Struggled to keep even a tiny portion of the image. All she really remembered was a black and white tile floor. The pattern, repeated over and over, stretching to dark brown walls. *Wavy blue light. Blue columns. Think. Think. Blue columns. Wavy light. Tile floor.*

Another ripple in reality, a sucking sensation, a giant pull, and Macari tumbled out of the odd cold and onto something unyielding. Her legs collapsed and she crumpled to the ground, a spasm burning up one leg while her shoulder hit a surface so hard she bounced. She skidded to a halt against something cold and winced.

She lay for a moment, trying to let her body adjust to all the sensations. The air, instantly oppressive, sticky, and sweet. The atmosphere heavy with vapor, like before a thunderstorm. Heat poured over her, from the hard surface below her to what felt like a blazing sun above. Only the wall behind her felt cool. She took quick inventory of her body. Ankle, definitely sprained. Cuts, bruises, maybe burns. Hands, burnt from the artifact.

The artifact. Macari groaned. It had followed her into the window, but it wasn't in her hand. It wasn't on the floor. *Gone. Again.*

Tears welled as reality set in. Everything hurt. The artifact refused to bond with her. She'd never complete her mission. Never go home. And wherever she'd landed felt foreign and full of hostile power and emotion. It pressed in on her mind, jiggled locks buried deep inside. New doors popped in to contain emotions she couldn't name. Feelings embedded in the floor, the walls.

What is this place?

Cautiously, she examined the surroundings. In front of her, the window wavered in midair, the dance floor of the club visible within its watery wavering depths. Through it, she could see the rest of the room as well, though as the scene faded and sharpened in front of her it obscured bits. Enormous blue columns extended from the black and white tile floor up until they faded to darkness. Each column butted up against another to form one solid circle. The columns appeared to be made of some sort of glass, and inside she sensed liquid, as well as fish and other animal life. At the bottom, a heavy layer of rock anchored plants of various types. Each column exuded power to varying degrees. *Water.* She studied them. No space between them to squeeze through. No way to get out.

Trapped.

In the center of each column, a dark shadow lingered, as though someone passed behind it or through it. She crossed the room to get a better look. A ghostly woman floated, her eyes bulged wide, her mouth open in a silent scream. Hair billowed around her. She hung suspended, toes scraping the rocks, fish darting around her. Macari gasped in horror, clapping hands to her mouth to stop the scream. She looked at the next column. Another woman. Every column, a woman. Thirteen in all, a tight circle of ghostly, dead women floating in water.

Macari spun, taking them all in. It was the only thing to see, apart from a simple metal chair that rested in the middle of a sunken portion of the floor in the very center of the room. Symbols surrounded the chair, etched into the tile. She ran her hand along it, looking for any weakness. The chair was solid, metal, bolted to the floor. She brushed her feet over the symbols, feeling some lingering power within them. Nothing active. *Yet. Why in the stars is this here?*

The window in front of her wavered, and a long leg poked out, followed by the rest of a male body.

Preacher.

As he emerged, Preacher leered at her. "Alone at last." He flicked a hand at the window and it dissolved down to nothing and vanished.

No escape.

The heavy air and the lust pouring from the man screamed at her to get out. She pictured The Edge in her mind, as clear as she could given the sudden jumping of her nerves and pulse, and tried to travel. Something blocked her.

The man laughed. "Don't think I can't feel that. I know what you are. And this place is perfect for someone like you." He gestured around at the columns. "Water trumps Air any day, especially in this place. This isn't just *any* water. It's blessed by Ancients. And beyond is thick earth, so wide and deep you could never shift enough Air to tunnel out. The only people who could travel here are those who know where it is, who have Earth and Water. And that, my angel, isn't you."

After the overload in the club, her power was sluggish and slow to respond, but she tried anyway. Macari focused energy around her as a shield, but found it weak. She struggled to strengthen it, but it remained a poor substitute of what it normally was. Her pulse pounded as she backed away from the man.

"What is this? A trinket, from an angel? Or the hand of the devil himself?" The man smiled, an expression that failed to meet his eyes or warm anything on his face. He held his hand up, with the artifact between his fingers. "Such a pretty thing. I wonder what it does. Oh wait, I already know. Quite the display you put on. Don't worry. All will be forgiven. I can cleanse you of sin. I can save you."

Preacher played with the stone, weaving it in between his fingers.

"Save me? From what?" Macari shifted to her left. The man moved a step forward, cutting her off.

"Yourself. Look at you. When you showed up, you had obviously been in sin. Now you've put on new clothes, but a wolf in new clothes is still a wolf, right?" He grinned, his teeth reminding her of dogs she'd seen. "Or, in this case, whore. You wear whore's clothes, after all."

"You can't hold me here." She shifted back to her left, feeling the column behind her. It held power, but not Air. She couldn't exactly pull on it, but she shouldn't need to. Frustrated, she tugged again at her own inner strength but found it sluggish and lackluster. Like it tunneled through something deep and dense to get to her. Like she usually felt around water.

Preacher watched her as she examined her surroundings, a satisfied look on his face. He licked his lips, clearly thinking he had the upper hand.

He might be right.

"That sounds like a challenge. I accept." He smiled again, then studied the stone. "It's quite fascinating. I can feel the heat and power. But nothing like before. I wonder how you unleashed it?"

I didn't. She could tell, even from this distance, that the artifact remained as shielded as it had been. Maybe she'd created another small crack, but it wasn't bonded. Which meant it could bond with anyone. She swallowed.

He tossed it up in the air and caught it as though it were a toy. "No matter. A question for another time." He turned to the nearest column and grinned. "I'll just store it for safe keeping."

Preacher moved the hand holding the stone toward the column, and then through the glass, his arm parting it as though it were no barrier at all. When his hand was fully submersed, he opened his fist and let the artifact fall. It drifted slowly to the bottom where it settled in among other stones.

He turned back to her and advanced toward her, close enough she could smell his breath. It smelled like the air in the club.

"It's not a challenge." She shifted again. He moved closer.

"It's time to admit that there's power greater than you. Greater than all of us. Kneel with me, your sins will be forgiven." He held out a hand, in a beseeching manner. But the emotion behind the gesture struck her like a brick. *Desire. Lust. Superiority. Domination.*

His other hand shifted, as though he scratched his leg. She followed the movement until he brought up a fist, obviously holding something. She tested the air, but so far he'd used no magic, no energy at all.

"I have something that will help you reach out for the spirit. Once you taste this, you'll beg me to save you. You'll be stripped and laid bare of all your inhibitions. And you. Will. Be. Mine."

The man raised his fist, and just as he did, something glinted in a column behind him. Her eyes flicked to the movement in the column. Preacher lunged, knocking her off her feet before she could do anything but cry out. Something sharp and wet hit her neck, and her mind sank down, down, down, into darkness.

CHAPTER EIGHTEEN

The gurgle of water tempted Macari from blackness. It giggled and tickled her feet, splashed her ankles, made her skin itch. Her head throbbed in time to the gurgles, or maybe it was her pulse. She couldn't stop the moan that followed, nor the coughing fit, which made her head hurt even more. Her hands moved reflexively to her face, or tried to. Something held them down. She tried to open her eyes, but the lids were so heavy. A taste lingered in her mouth, like the metallic taste of blood.

On instinct, she tried to focus power around her as a cloak or shield, but couldn't reach it. *Head. Fuzzy.* Her magic floated just out of reach, maddeningly distant.

A surge of curiosity and lust reached her before any sounds or footsteps. Someone watched her, and even though she couldn't actively access her power, it seemed she was able to read emotions. Reading emotions on the air was as automatic as breathing for her. Macari focused on it, the one thing that seemed to be working. *Arrogance. Satisfaction.* It came from somewhere to her left, a bit distant.

He didn't move. He didn't speak. Her pulse pounded. *Open your eyes, Macari. You have to open your eyes.* After a fight, she managed to get her eyes open, though at first she couldn't raise her head to look anywhere but the floor. What she saw beneath her feet was bad enough.

Water. A lot of water, with the metal chair legs sunk in the middle of it, her bare feet dangling.

He'd bound her ankles to the chair legs with a weave of water. She could see the dark blue translucent bands around her wrists as well. Her skirt had been arranged around her legs, high up on the thigh. Underneath it, her bare flesh stuck to the chair. The underwear Anna had given her was gone. Some sort of metal rod lay on the chair between her thighs. It wasn't touching her, but it looked like it was supposed to.

Metal? Why so much metal?

She didn't think she wanted the answer. Water, and earth, working together? *Why?*

Macari raised her eyes, trying to see beyond the limited circle around her feet. The water columns obscured anything that might be beyond them. Each was illuminated by a dim internal light that reached up through the water to put the contents on display. Fish floated around in most of them, gurgling, happy fish that teased and taunted each floating dead girl. The whole thing cast an eerie glow that turned her stomach.

She closed her eyes again, took a deep breath. Then another. Focused on her body, on trying to push Air through her veins in a way that would clear the fog from her mind. While she still couldn't manipulate most of her energies, it did seem to help. A tiny bit. Another deep breath. Two. Three. Finally, with another deep intake of air she managed to lift her head and open her eyes.

Something beyond the columns to her right shifted. A quick intake of breath. *Excitement.* She turned to stare at the area, but all she could make out was a shadow behind the shadows, a darkening of the water in certain areas of the column not obscured by fish or girl.

As she watched, the shadow grew larger and larger, until it became vaguely human shaped. It shifted to the center of the column, and the floating girl within moved backward, out of sight. Then the shadow grew larger, and a foot stepped out, followed by arms and the rest of the body.

Preacher.

She pulled in another deep breath. *Stars, I need my power.* She twisted an arm, but her hands remained tightly bound. If she could just grasp her focus, she could remove the air from the water binding. It would disintegrate. Water without air was nothing. Certainly no threat.

Neither am I. Not now.

Preacher stepped to the edge of her circle and stopped. Smiled. His eyes traveled the length of her body, lingering on the metal rod placed between her thighs. He licked his lips.

"I'm glad you're awake. There's so much to talk about. You… you're the gift I've been waiting for." He sat down on the floor in front of her, near the edge of the pool underneath her chair, crossing his legs in a comfortable pose.

"What is this place? Who are you, really?" Macari couldn't make the words louder than a whisper. Her throat cracked, her lips so dry they burned.

Preacher smiled, a movement that lit his eyes with manic fire. "Your salvation. And mine. I've waited so long for someone like you. I'm a patient man, but even I must admit these last months have tried even my patience. So much potential in that place, so much sin, so much for me to do, and yet the one I truly sought eluded me. But not anymore. Here you are." He rubbed one thigh with the palm of his hand.

"You don't know me."

"I know *of* you. I knew it when I tasted your power. When you dropped into the den of sin as a shining star among swine. You're an angel, fallen from heaven. And through you we will both reach salvation. Though any such journey is not without hardship. You must be cleansed back to your true form."

"My true form?" *What form? What does he think I am?*

His eyes danced, and he stared at her crotch as though he thought something might crawl out from between her thighs. "You should never have been there, though I suppose I understand why you were. Such a place would corrupt any innocent creature.

But no fear." He stood up, making her throw her head back in alarm. He smiled, almost gently. "I can make you better."

Preacher walked around her chair until he was behind her. She sensed him back there. His body heat and energy caressed the back of her neck. His emotions licked at her mind. *Lust. Greed. Domination. Power.* Her mind took them all in, shoved them behind the appropriate doors. Doors that bulged, doors that balked. She didn't *want* these feelings. They lived in the deepest part of her, the darkest part. A part she didn't truly know. Didn't *want* to know.

More deep breaths. *If I can just clear this poison from my system, I can focus power and escape.* She'd never encountered anyone like this man. He seemed unhinged, like someone who'd nearly overloaded on magic but remained somehow conscious and capable. Everything about his looks said he was cool and composed, normal. But he couldn't hide his true self from her, and he seemed to know it. *He likes it. He likes the feel of my power.*

Like Anna, he must have sensed power when he touched her skin. Even unconscious he'd felt it. And he wanted to feel it again.

She thought about it. *If he touched me, I could exchange with him. I could get my strength back.* She couldn't focus enough to exchange over a distance but if he touched her, she could. *I think.* The contact would make it possible. *Then I could* bind him with Air.

"Shall we begin?" The whisper in her ear turned her stomach. Macari strained against the water bindings. Her head lolled to one side with the effort. She couldn't see him. She smelled him:

a mix of lust, drink, sweat. He pulled his fingers through her hair slowly like he touched something precious. She strained to make a connection, but simply touching her hair wasn't enough. She wanted to scream in frustration but the only sound that emerged was a hiccup.

He backed away, body heat retreating with his breath. A slurping, sucking sound. Footsteps. She detected a shadow through the columns to her left now. The artifact glinted innocently at her.

The footsteps stopped, and for a moment the only sound she heard was the gurgling water. Then, a loud click.

A thousand needles burned their way from her feet up through her body, into her mind. She tried to scream as white heat raced through her veins. The room blurred. Plinks of water vibrated against her ears, dripped down her face, soaked her skirt. The water was cold, so cold, it hurt everywhere it touched. Sizzling sounds, a hum that ripped at her soul. Wave after wave of misery. The stench of burned flesh and hair. Her thoughts scattered.

Magic leaked out. Her ability to sense emotions magnified. *Lust. Joy. Excitement. Anticipation.* All obviously his, tainted by his smell. *Fear. Anguish. Panic. Despair. Not mine. Someone else. Several. Women.* All had sat in this chair, and all remained nearby, floating in the columns of water, surrounded by fish. He'd done to them what he did to her. Her mind took it all, raced it down the corridors of her mind. The doors weren't strong enough to contain so much dark, so much evil. It all raged in her mind.

It ended as abruptly as it had started. The jabs in her feet simply shut off, though lingering waves of heat continued up and down her legs, spine, arms, everywhere. All of the scattered feelings, which had overwhelmed her, vanished with it, fading into the background until only three vivid ones remained. Her despair. His lust. Her anger.

He's enjoying this.

The thought made her even more angry. Something else began to grow, something she wasn't accustomed to feeling. More than anger. More than frustration or fear or panic.

Hate.

In her mind, the doors in the darkest, deepest portion of the corridor jiggled. She struggled to keep them closed. *I can't let them out. They'll fuel him.* Like the people in the club, he'd use the excess to do something even worse. She couldn't let that happen. *Can't let them out. Lock! Keep them locked.*

She panted with the effort.

Somewhere distant, a rumble mixed with the gurgling water. Bubbles floated to the top, the water agitated by some unseen force. She focused on the bubbles. Tried to regain focus. Sharpen thoughts.

How can he do this? This isn't just murder. This is…evil. Maybe that's why Mother didn't care about the murders. She knew it could be worse. Much worse.

The planes had been split to save humans from this. It obviously hadn't worked. They hadn't been saved from themselves.

Footsteps drew her out of her own body and thoughts and into awareness of the prison. The columns full of water looked as though they were boiling, bubbles racing furiously from the bottom. One in particular had turned a slight orange hue, making the girl's face within glow as though she danced in an unseen flame.

Macari stared at the water. Preacher pushed into the column, merged with it like a drop of water merges with the ocean, then popped out the other side without a drop of water on him. She gaped at him. *He passed through water. And glass.* Was it all an illusion? His power let him walk in and out as easily as if he walked through air, passing through a seemingly solid object.

I can't do that.

Panic rose in her throat. She swallowed it down. *Not now.*

Between the pain and whatever he'd done to her before, her thoughts remained fuzzy and disjointed. She cringed as he drew closer to her, his stench and lust leeching onto her as though she'd rolled in mud.

He circled around to stroke her hair. "Oh, you are all that I hoped for and more. My precious, precious angel. You are my salvation, and I shall have you." He crooned, as a parent reassuring an infant. "Not now. No, no…we must wait for the right moment. You are not yet ready. I sense that you still fight. When you beg me to touch you, then we'll be ready."

He bent toward her, his lips next to her ear. "Are you ready for me to touch you? Would you like that?"

Her nose wrinkled against the odor he wore like a suit.

She couldn't work her lips, much less her tongue. No moisture, though the surrounding air was loaded with it, her mouth remained bone dry.

"I know you'd like it. When you're ready, really ready, then I will take you to the heights where you can be cleansed of all your misdeeds. Together we'll be one and achieve true glory. Together. Patience, my angel. Another cleansing I think."

He stepped away, his footsteps fading to the left. She saw once again his shadow as he circled around the outside of the water tubes. Now she knew how he'd done it before. There was no way out behind her, not the way he did it. She'd have to destroy those things to get past them. Filled with water, she could do it if her strength returned. She could expand the air inside the columns until they exploded. She'd relish the chance.

As soon as I get focus. As soon as...I...clear...thoughts.

The click of something metallic, followed by a thousand knives cutting from the inside, shattered her thoughts and exploded her mind.

CHAPTER NINETEEN

This time, when her mind returned, she could tell it had been more than just a few minutes. Her back was stiff and her neck throbbed from being in one position too long. *How long was I out?* It could have been hours. Days. No sun or stars cycled to tell her how long. The mark on her hand barely darkened the skin. *Is it lighter than it was when I got here?*

Preacher's hands caressed her hair. Her skirt had been moved, up past her hips, exposing everything below to the open air. Her breasts poked out from the remnants of her blouse. He'd drawn a few runes on her thighs. She couldn't make them out, her vision was too blurry. They held no power over her, but the thought that he'd touched her naked body while her mind was vacant filled her with disgust. A feeling she couldn't hide, nor keep from seeping into the atmosphere. It only seemed to excite him.

Her arms felt sticky. The pungent scent of olives surrounded her.

Behind her, Preacher sighed. His breath moved the hair on her neck. "Are you ready for me?"

Macari couldn't bring herself to speak. Her thoughts swirled, incoherent. She just wanted him gone. *Gone. Gone. Gone.*

Water in the tubes boiled. Most of them had turned reddish orange now, though one stood out among the rest, bright red in its fury. She focused on it, drawn by the color and the anger and by something that glinted at the bottom.

The artifact.

If I can connect with it…if I can reach it. Unlock it. I could use its power rather than my own. It contained all the power of the Fire Ancient himself. All she had to do was bond with it.

Fire needs Air in order to burn.

Maybe if she fed it what little Air she could muster, it would be enough. It was cracked already. Perhaps she could leverage it open.

I need to let go.

She tried to lick her lips, but there was no moisture on her tongue. *Let go. Stop hiding from myself. Stop locking doors. Let go of everything. Every bottled emotion, every feeling I've siphoned from others.*

Lay her heart bare. Here, in this room, with this deranged, evil, twisted…

I can't.

Preacher chuckled. "Not quite, I see. Good, because the longer the journey, the greater the salvation. The more wonder and joy at destination's end. A little encouragement, that's all you need. Here, my dove. Let us anoint you. Soon, you'll be ready."

She felt him move. Shift something. A shadow fell over her head from above. Thick liquid poured down over her, saturating her hair, face, body. It dripped into her eyes. She clamped them shut. It drooled onto her lips and into her mouth. It tasted sweet. *Like berries, but wrong.* It had a bitter aftertaste she didn't understand. Her stomach turned.

The liquid kept coming. More and more of it cascaded over her head and continued down her body. It consumed her breasts. Infiltrated her navel.

Preacher reached his arm across to trickle more of it over her groin. He panted as it pooled on the chair between her legs. He brought his mouth close to her exposed body and blew. She jerked, straining to get away. Hating the thick feel of the liquid. The smell. The way it heated up when Preacher breathed on it.

Preacher sighed. His excitement reached a fever pitch, and he threw the container aside. It clanged and rolled to a stop near one of the columns. Preacher moved slowly around, bending as close as he could without putting his feet in the pool of water. He breathed on her breasts, her neck, her eyes. Everywhere his breath touched grew hot as though he'd brushed her with fire.

It's not magic. It's not...please stop. Please.

She whimpered, unable to make her lips form a word.

Preacher smiled, and moved behind her chair. She heard cloth shift, and smelled flesh and the heavy scent of a man in heat. She heard something slap, a squishing sound, more slapping. Preacher shifted, and in her peripheral vision she could see him as his hands stroked his penis. He'd used the oil to coat himself as well. His hands and member were slick with oil and sweat. His eyes fastened on her thighs and groin. He licked his lips.

As he stroked, his eyes grew wide, lit with insane glee. He moved his hand faster, grunting with effort. He threw his head back and yelled his climax, a primal sound that echoed around the enclosure. He ejaculated onto her, his semen uniting with the oil on her thighs. She watched it trickle down the sides of her legs, numb, as he coaxed more fluid from the tip of his penis.

When he finished, he ran his finger through the puddle between her thighs. He brought it up to his nose and inhaled deeply. She stared as he licked each finger one at a time. When he began to caress his penis again, she focused on the column of boiling water, instead of his face, and fought the urge to throw up. Her stomach roiled at the stench, lust, and heat.

Focus. Focus on the artifact. Lasair. Please. Help me. Let me in. I need help. Please.

Tarian's voice sounded as clear as though the woman stood right next to her. *You have to let go. That's what I had to do.*

Preacher softly stroked himself a few more times as he smiled at her. His face wore a wide, innocent expression that frightened her more than anything he'd done so far. He licked his lips. "You have been anointed. You have been bathed in the holy essence, given to me by God. I will share it with you, and through you we shall both reach true and lasting salvation. Are you ready for me now, sweet one?"

She refused to look at him. Refused to even try to lift her head. All of her concentration focused on the artifact, so close and yet so far away. She could almost feel it. Almost sense it reaching for her.

Fire needs Air in order to burn.

It needs me.

Tears fell then. They rolled down her cheeks and splashed on the chair between her thighs, where the metal rod still waited, shimmering.

Preacher turned and walked slowly to the empty column and through it.

Another click.

She knew nothing more.

CHAPTER TWENTY

The stink of Preacher's breath behind her made her tense every muscle in her body as she regained consciousness. His hands lovingly caressed her greasy, wet hair, and he whispered in her ear, though she had no idea what he was saying or how long he'd been there. Her bones ached. Even her natural healing failed to stifle the effects of whatever it was he did to her. A tiny voice in the back of her mind told her he was right. She'd beg him to touch her. Beg him to do anything besides send another round of fire through her veins. She'd nearly reached her threshold. Her control on herself, nearly gone.

I'm. Never. Going. Home.

She felt power from the artifact, just out of reach, hidden by a haze of pain and fog. All of the columns boiled red, now. Ironic. *All this time it's been a dead thing. Now that I have nothing left. Now. It opens up. To bond. With who? Him?*

The only one in the room truly open to who he was. Despair settled in her heart and squeezed tears from her eyes. *He'll have fire. Nothing will stop him. I'll be floating in water soon.*

I hate water.

Preacher appeared not to notice the building power or the boiling water, or if he did, he didn't care. *Maybe he thinks his salvation caused it.*

Her own mortality had never entered her mind before. She was daemon. All daemon lived for centuries. Their lifespan was measured in turns of the stars. They existed until their energy released into the atmosphere for others to claim, for the last time. Their magic held them together far beyond a human lifespan.

But this...her body couldn't combat this. Her power, so stirred up by his treatments or cleansing was scattered, erratic, loose around the edges. Intention formed the basis and she simply couldn't pull it together. Not anymore. Agony and fear were all she could focus, now.

"Sweet, sweet angel, are you ready for me?"

Macari lifted her head slightly, her eyes taking in the room. Could it really look the same? She felt so different, so used, that she couldn't believe her surroundings remained as they'd been. Same columns of water filled with dead women. Same puddle of water below her, same metal chair. Same human man with the same lust. Same, same, same.

"Not quite. Not quite. I understand. The journey is long, and hard, and I am worthy. I must work for it. I must..." Preacher's voice trailed off as he moved. "Once more, sweet one."

Pain. Black.

Nothing.

CHAPTER TWENTY-ONE

Black circled. Pushed. Teased. Like the inky void of night. The emptiness of the vortex on the Corsaerie. It expanded, so vast it dwarfed everything. Violated only by small, white flecks of light. Macari watched as they moved, formed patterns, shifted, formed new ones. She wanted to touch one. It seemed vital that she touch one. But they were so far away. So very far away. And her body...

Do I even have a body?

Dimly, awareness returned. It crept over her like a lover crawling into bed. She noticed the cramps in her neck, first. Her head slumped so far down she nearly couldn't breathe. Pain behind her eyes, next. It throbbed, each pulse another insult. Searing heat along her thighs as though she'd been cut a thousand times.

Despair circulated through her veins instead of blood. She kept her eyes closed and let it. Felt it. Experienced every bit of it. Didn't try to lock it up, or hide it. Not even from herself. She deserved to feel it. She owned it. Preacher couldn't take it from her. Couldn't torture it out of her. The thought brought a strange sense of comfort. No matter what he did, he couldn't touch the parts of her mind that formed her soul, her existence.

Somehow, despair changed into something she didn't quite understand at first. *Determination.* She let it feed her soul. She heard him breathing, just behind her. *He's waiting for me to wake up.*

She remained still, eyes closed, while she continued to take inventory. Water covered her feet. Water gurgled in the columns. The Fire Artifact waited in one of them, expectant. Its power licked at her, like tongues of flame. An invitation. A seeking.

Fire needs Air in order to burn.

He can't have it. He can't have the artifact. I have to bond with it, before he does. Come on, Macari. You are daemon! You can do this. You can reach out and bond with the stone. You just have to…

Have…to…

Let go.

In her mind, the corridor took shape. Closed doors extended further than she remembered.

No more doors.

She opened one near the surface. Joy. It radiated out to mix with Preacher's own. He must have felt it, because he breathed a hot sigh along the back of her neck and whispered. "Ah, angel, you make me so happy. I can feel you. Truly feel you, as I've never felt before. I know you *know* me, and it's…amazing."

Preacher leaned in close, his breath making her gag. "I know you hear me. Are you ready?"

She licked her lips, though it did nothing. Took as deep a breath as she could muster. Breathed out one word. "Yes."

She sensed delight at the word, excitement, anticipation.

She let them run through her mind and used them to unlock the corresponding doors, letting go of all that she'd held inside. Delight, excitement, anticipation rushed out, magnified. Preacher giggled. Macari's heart raced as the absurd sound lifted her spirits.

Preacher ran his fingers through her hair one more time, then stepped away. He circled the chair until he stood in front of her, his feet on the edge of the pool of water. A smile stretched across his face, contorting his cheeks.

She unlocked affection. Hope.

Preacher's eyes widened as the feelings reached him. He clasped his hands together and chortled. She readied herself for more torture. Instead he circled the chair, a lion stalking his prey. Around them, water seethed in the columns.

She hesitated then. Several doors remained. Darker doors. Doors held by enormous power and strength of will. If she opened them, no telling the consequences.

And if I don't?

She felt the artifact reach for her. It enticed. Welcomed. Encouraged. A thin filament of red and gold extended through the column and into the air, like long fingers that searched for treasure. The band of fire split around Preacher and snaked its way toward her. When it touched her forehead, she sensed Lasair. All of his longing, desire, despair, yearning. And something much more powerful than all of that.

The most powerful emotion of all. The one she kept locked at the very back of the corridor. Behind hate. Behind hope. Beyond contempt, disgust. The one thing she couldn't feel for this tortured soul in front of her. But the one thing Lasair felt above all else, and the one thing that might save her.

Love.

If she let it go, she'd have nothing left to give. Her soul would be laid bare before this madman. And her plan might not work. To be able to break his hold on her, she needed him to touch her. Flesh to flesh. Even if she opened every door, it might not be enough to bond the stone. It might shift to Preacher anyway. He'd be an insane, frenzied human in possession of more power than she could defeat.

The stone would bond with someone willing to accept it fully. Which of them was more willing? More accepting? Which of them had laid their innermost selves bare before the power of Fire?

No choice. No other way.

Though the idea of his skin on hers filled her with dread, she longed for it. *If he touches me, we could exchange. If he touches me, I'd be able to disperse it. I don't want him to touch me. But if he touches me, I could bond with everything. Everything in the room...*

Her thoughts went in circles. *Touch, don't touch, touch, feel, touch.* She shook her head, a slow move from side to side that did little to clear her mind. Deep breath. More breath. More air. Deep breath.

She opened the last door.

Love poured out, a tidal wave of feeling so powerful she might have been in the deepest ocean, tumbling in a surge of waves, or tossed by a hurricane through the wind. She gulped, and hiccupped, a move which heightened Preacher's excitement. He embraced the feelings she'd turned loose and tears streamed down his face.

"My angel." His voice, filled with awe. He waved a hand, and a stepping-stone rose in the water in front of her feet. He knelt on it, his hands hovering just over her thighs.

He's going to touch me, he's going to touch me, touch me, touch.
Macari moaned.

Preacher licked his lips, a bit of saliva lodged in the corner of his mouth. He picked up the metal rod that still lay between her thighs. He ran his fingers up and down it. It was the caress of a man tracing the curves of his lover's body.

Touch me, touch me, touch. She pressed the thoughts into his mind as she would any daemon. Willing him to hear her. Willing him to obey.

Preacher shifted his body forward, one hand on the metal chair between her thighs. With the other hand, he held the rod pointed at her, then lowered it to her thighs, in between, pushed it forward.

She shifted, her thighs squishing in the pools of oily water, squelching in a sound that wasn't natural, wasn't normal, wasn't anything she ever wanted to hear again. She avoided the metal even as she leaned for his touch. *Touch me, touch me, touch me.* She tried to clear her throat, which came out more as a grunt. She managed two more words. "Touch. Me."

CHAPTER TWENTY-TWO

Preacher beamed, radiant with excitement and joy. Lust, and the scent of release flooded over her body. She tried to smile. He moved closer, leaning in, the tip of the rod touching her underneath the skirt, right on the soft folds of her skin. It felt strangely cold.

Preacher shifted his legs apart. His penis poked through the opening of his pants. He raised his empty hand and made a fist. Bit into it, then released with a sigh. He lowered his hand. She watched it fall. Traced the movement with her gaze until his fingers came to rest on her bare thigh.

As his skin made contact with hers, she thrust every bit of energy she could muster into him. Willed it to connect with his core. His eyes widened as he felt her power invade his. His mouth twisted. Excitement flared. Macari pulled it in, drawing lust, excitement, and yearning along with it. She let it all overtake her, join with the anger and despair from herself and from every woman who'd been tortured in this room. She wove it into an integrated whole.

She let his filth and evil slide through her mind and back out. No more doors. No more locking it away. She became a conduit and an amplifier.

From him, she took the ability to focus. Each breath brought more, and more brought the ability to solidify her intentions. Soon, though their bodies hadn't moved an inch, their power mingled in a full-on exchange.

She opened to the air around them and to any residual energy residing there. With Preacher in thrall to the exchange, she reached far enough to grasp the tiny bits from fish. She pulled it all in, sent it through Preacher as he gasped and twitched. His body rocked, his hand cemented to her thigh. His other hand dropped the metal rod and his eyes rolled back into his head as waves of euphoria descended. He didn't damper, he didn't shield, he didn't respond in any way. He simply took all she gave and in doing so, gave her far more in return.

He gave her the ability to fight back.

With his power combined with her own, she wove a bridge to the column where the artifact danced in boiling red water. She fanned the artifact with Air.

The water flared, transformed into a column of fire that roared through the tubes. The glass shattered in an explosion of water, fish, and bits of debris. Water cascaded out over the floor, bearing fish and the bodies of dead women. The girls collapsed into heaps, arms splayed, eyes wide. Fire billowed out, filled the room, and gathered them all up into its embrace.

The shackles on Macari's arms and legs melted into the pool below.

She barely felt it. Barely felt the heat. Didn't feel it burn her skin or her clothes. She was so caught up in the flood of power that awareness had taken a back seat. Her mind swirled with it. The room danced around her, a kaleidoscope of flame and water, air and earth.

The acrid odor of burned flesh and smoldering hate filled her nostrils and shook her out of the mind lock.

Overload. Must. Stop.

If she couldn't cut the flow, she'd die here. Nobody would ever know. She fumbled with control, trying to locate the external source of power to shield it. Not from Preacher. She'd used all he possessed and more. Fed it to the Air, where it fanned the artifact into a frenzy. She searched for the stone. Impossible. The heat had created vapor with the water from the columns and turned the room into a steam bath full of dead things.

The power. It's coming from somewhere. Find the source, Macari. Find the source. She slowed her breath and concentrated on the stream that curled around her. Traced it to the source. Startled, she realized the power flowed from within, not without.

It's me. It's all me.

Stop. Macari. Stop!

She screamed. In the scream, she found her center of focus. She released the exchange and Preacher collapsed. He fell backward, his upper body falling into the pool of water while his legs and feet remained on the platform he'd created. Her body vibrated from so much exertion on top of so much pain, and she huddled on the floor, panting, as the sounds of collapse died down around her. It was then she heard it, the scraping of something on the floor.

Preacher uttered a guttural sound; half-laugh, half-moan, and brought the stone up to his lips and kissed it. Fire had taken his hair and burned his clothes to fragments. His skin was red and raw. His expression, so reverent, so at odds with who she knew this man to be, made giggles rise into Macari's throat. She choked on them and coughed, in near hysterics. Giggles rose again, cutting off her breath. She bent, resting her hands on her thighs, trying to catch her breath and gain control of herself.

"I can feel it! I can feel salvation. You've brought it to me."

Macari looked up. Preacher stared at the rock in his hands, and Macari stared too. It glowed, at first a faint pulse, then a steady stream that matched her giggles and coughs. She tried to stop, but it only brought tears to her eyes. They streamed down her cheeks. She gave up the attempt to control her emotions and simply let them out, let the tears fall, and let the pain do what it would to her body.

The rock flamed, a towering sheet of fire reflected in Preacher's dark eyes. He laughed, delighted. His lust evaporated. As elation took hold, his eyes widened, then his hands began to glow too, a bright orange-red. He screamed, his hands outstretched in front of him. The color raced up his arms and into his face, as though a fire had been set to his skin. His scream turned to a primal shout. His body jerked, twitched, and danced in a macabre display.

Macari watched, horrified, as Preacher's body melted. His skin detached and wrapped around itself, exposing his internal organs. Blood sizzled and boiled in his veins, then evaporated, turning the air to red mist. The scent of burnt flesh filled the room. She retched as it invaded her senses.

As Macari threw up bile and acid, Preacher's voice faded, the glow faded, his emotions and life force faded, and then he was gone. Nothing left but bones, bits of blood, and the stone.

She didn't move. Couldn't. Her body froze, locked in place by horror and an overuse of power. She held her breath until blackness threatened to take her and then she gasped, air rushing in, burning her lungs. She knelt in a pool of filth, and stared. Drained. Empty. Beyond feeling anything at all.

CHAPTER TWENTY-THREE

Macari wasn't sure how long she knelt in the room. How long she spent staring at the remains of Preacher. How long she locked her gaze on each corpse. Each woman. Once someone's daughter. Or mother. She might have knelt there a day. Or ten days. She might never have moved again, except something caught her eye. Something flickered, and moved.

She blinked several times, then rubbed her eyes to clear the crust and film from them. Squinted to see what movement could possibly exist. Surely nothing had survived the scorching fire and raging heat.

The Fire Artifact glinted in the horrible light. It rocked, back and forth in a pool of blood and dead fish, until it worked up momentum and began to roll. It moved across the floor toward her like it knew exactly where it wanted to be. It came to rest beside her foot. Red and gold flashed in brilliant sparks of color as though it were a live flame that simply flickered into existence, no kindling required.

Macari picked it up. Its size had diminished by half. What once had been a craggy black rock was now a polished oblong gem formed of something blood red, with orange, blue, and yellow strands running through it. The surface was smooth, as though polished in the heat of a thousand suns. It was the most beautiful thing she'd ever seen.

She turned it over. Just beneath the red surface a deep shadow formed the symbol for Fire. Even the symbol seemed to burn.

It belonged to her, now. And she to it. Through her connection, she felt Lasair himself. She'd bonded with it, and in doing so, with him.

What took you so long?

She didn't answer, but he didn't seem to expect one. She felt his hope and satisfaction before he withdrew. They didn't need words. Feeling spoke louder anyway.

She licked her lips. It didn't help. They were cracked and raw, but her mouth had no moisture to give them. She took in a deep, shuddering breath then heaved as the smell in the room broke through her shock and exhaustion. Her body shook so hard she nearly dropped the stone. Clutching the artifact, she pushed herself to unsteady feet and backed away from Preacher's body until she hit a wall.

Heavy bricks formed the bulk of the room. Desperate to get out, she used the wall for support and worked her way around the circular space. Dim electric bulbs here and there along the wall provided the only light. No door. No window.

No way out.

She fought the rising panic and forced herself to take a deep breath, then choked again on the death and decay in the room. Heaved. Swallowed bile. Heaved again. Sweat poured down the side of her face. She raised the artifact to her forehead. She didn't think it would help, but it did. Somehow, she found enough calm to take a deep breath without gagging. Then another. She counted each. *One. Two. Three. Four.*

Slowly, her pulse returned to normal. She tried not to think about where she was. Deep beneath the surface, buried in earth. So far away from air and wind that she couldn't even sense them. She had only what she brought with her, and it was precious little after everything that had happened.

Preacher had warned her that she wouldn't be able to travel. Earth and Water were needed to enter or exit this space. She had neither.

But now that Preacher's hold on the room was gone and she'd bonded with the artifact, perhaps Fire and Air would be enough.

Macari glanced at the mark on her hand. It had nearly faded into non-existence. She had little time left, and one question remained to satisfy her mission. And only one person could answer it. *Preacher didn't travel the way I do. Maybe I can jump from here to someplace familiar.*

She focused, taking her time to weave the intent, entice it from her very last reserves, and funnel it into the artifact. The stone responded and offered a boost. Macari closed her eyes. Pictured where she wanted to go. And traveled.

This time when she landed, Macari's feet touched sand, instead of water. She stood near the ocean, on the spot where she'd met Tarian. Moonlight high overhead told her that at least a day had passed since she'd been here. Maybe more. She'd no way of knowing how long she'd been with Preacher.

She might have been sitting there for weeks, staring at each dead woman in turn. She'd burned their pale, tortured faces in her memory. One day, when she had time, she'd seek each of them on the Wind. She'd like to remember them from before Preacher had tarnished their lives and taken their souls. She'd find a scene where each was happy and still full of life and burn that as a memory, instead.

Macari held the artifact carefully between her fingers. In the moonlight, it pulsated a warm red glow.

Time to lock you up. No sneaking away from me again! Now, where to hide you?

Macari checked her dress, or what was left of it. The top had been slit to her navel. *Perfect.* She pressed the stone into the indentation of flesh. It wedged into place, protruding slightly. But it would hold firm with a little help. She pulled air both from herself and from nature and wove a tight net to keep the stone in place. It would provide an invisible, impenetrable barrier.

As she sewed, she tickled the stone with a bit of air and used its own power to formulate the weave. When she finished, it lay secure beneath a spider's web of air so intricate that it would be impossible to remove. The stone's power wasn't blocked, but it wouldn't fall off her body either.

"I thought I asked you not to do that here." Tarian's voice, amused, sounded from the rocks above.

Macari turned, letting her shirt drop back into place. "You said not to unlock it here. I didn't. But you also said I could count on you if I needed help. I hope that was true."

Tarian stepped carefully down the pathway, Alex at her side. He exuded annoyance, frustration, concern, and curiosity all at once. Macari couldn't help but smile and wonder who the concern was for. Her, or Tarian.

"You look like shit." Tarian said as she drew close enough to see Macari in the moonlight. "What happened?"

Macari looked down, and realized how disheveled she was. The skirt was burnt in places and splattered with blood. The shirt hung in tatters, her breasts exposed. Feet covered in filth and bits of…she didn't want to think about it. "I…" she couldn't think of how to begin. What to say. Or how to ask what she really wanted to know. Tears formed at the corners of her eyes and made a slow trail down her cheeks.

"You're welcome to come in. Rest. I'll get the healers." Tarian offered a hand.

Macari felt a pulse of power and realized the baby had kicked because she saw Tarian wince. She shook her head. "I don't have time. I only came to ask…it's just that to go home, I need to know." She paused to stare at Tarian's extended belly, unsure of how to ask without sounding rude.

Alex cleared his throat, and Tarian shifted. She glanced at Alex, then back at Macari. She rubbed her stomach, caressing the unborn child as she answered. "I did it to get a book that I thought would help save my family. And myself, to be honest. I did it as part of a deal with Ruarc. One joining in exchange for the *Book of Daemon*."

Macari closed her eyes, and felt for the first time since the quest had begun, the pull of the Court. Her mission, complete. When she opened her eyes, it was to find Tarian looking curiously at her.

"Did that help?"

"Yes." Macari smiled. "Thank you. I should go."

Tarian nodded. Macari sensed understanding beyond anything she deserved emanating from the woman.

Alex shook his head. "Wait. You got some explaining to do. You show up here, on a shielded beach, covered in blood and God knows what and then you just wanna vanish?"

"Alex, she's exhausted. She doesn't have to explain." Tarian sounded amused rather than irritated.

"Like hell." Alex pointed at Macari. "Look at her. Someone's been at her."

Macari took Alex's hand in hers and sent an image of the room where she'd left Preacher. When she finished, his eyes were so wide they nearly glowed in the darkness. "They…someone should take them home. I'm sure they had lives. And families. But it's bound by earth, and water. No doors."

"Good thing I'm good with rocks then."

Tarian stared curiously from Macari to Alex, but said nothing.

"I hope to come back. One day." She stared into Alex's eyes and smiled when she saw the flash of interest buried there under all the bravado and concern.

"I hope you do." Tarian stepped back to give Macari room.

Macari smiled at them both, dipped her head, then took the Corsaerie.

CHAPTER TWENTY-FOUR

Macari stepped out of the Wind onto the edge of the cliff overlooking Benata City. Exhilarated by successful travel through the Corsaerie, she tapped the stone embedded in her naval. *I can go back anytime I want. I can see how humans really live. I can see Alex, too.* The thought filled her with excitement.

Sunlight warmed her shoulders and bare breasts as she stood there, letting the mountain breeze play with the fragments of clothing that remained. She lifted her face to drink it in. *Home.*

In front of her, three Shee circled the Stulos as they always did. She bowed to them, and called "Honor to you! And my thanks."

She heard a giggle in response. Jasmine, always there, hardly ever seen. *"Air finds Fire, Fire finds flame. Change comes, Wind Walker."*

Macari grinned at the empty air. Then she turned to survey Benata City. She held out her hands and let her senses drift down to the city, down the walkways and paths, through the buildings.

She connected with the network of minds and hearts that existed there. She was too far away to detect any emotions on the air but she knew when she did, she'd let them flow through. She wouldn't cage them again.

She traveled to the court and paused just outside the arches to peer in. First Mother stood alone in the center. Sunlight streamed onto her face as she stood in quiet contemplation and waited for her daughter to report.

Regret at an indefinable loss filled her heart. *Why'd you do it, Mother? Why was it worth the risk?* Macari suffered so much to bring back two pieces of seemingly insignificant information. Why had her mother cared more for it than she did for her own daughter?

She started to gather focus to form mental shields. But then she stopped, and slowly let the shields drop.

No more hiding. No more shields.

If she'd survived the assault, then her mother could survive witnessing it. And, perhaps, understand what she'd done to her daughter. Maybe it would help her mother realize how foolish the quest had been.

Though if I'd never gone, I'd never have met Alex. And Tarian. And Anna.

She smiled at the thought of them. *Even if Alex felt wary around me, he still welcomed me. Still felt outrage when he saw how I'd been treated. They don't know me, yet they care for me.*

It's more than Mother showed. She set me an impossible task and cared nothing for the consequences.

Though humans had an immense capacity for evil, as Preacher had proved, they also had an even greater ability for love, friendship, and growth. *I'll make my report, then go back to visit. This time, without the mission or stress. This time, for me.*

Macari stepped inside the gazebo. Power rained down to connect her to the mind network within the structure. She waited, knowing that even if she never spoke a word, her mother would know all that had happened.

Her mother turned, opened her mouth to extend the greeting, then stopped. Her eyes widened as she took in Macari's disheveled appearance. Bruises had begun to form. Macari hadn't bothered to heal them, nor change her clothes. Her mother's eyes flicked down, past her daughter's exposed breasts to the navel decorated with a sparkling gem.

"Daughter. You are welcome." First Mother's voice was devoid of emotion. Calm. Forceful. Not to be denied.

"Am I?" Macari moved to a bench and sat down. "I'm not so sure, anymore."

Her mother didn't follow, but stood in the center, back stiff, hands clasped. She felt her mother's mental probe and closed her eyes as the events replayed in her mind from beginning to end. Every word, gesture, and flicker of emotion experienced as though for the first time.

Macari flinched at the first round of attack from Preacher. Her body flexed and twitched as she felt, again, the release of emotions that led to her bond with the Fire Artifact.

She noticed that her mother issued no response. No horror or shock at a daughter thus tortured. No concern regarding her daughter's health or well-being.

Macari lived through her final meeting with Tarian once again. *I traded Ruarc one joining for the Book of Daemon.* Her mother's eyes widened at the simple statement. Fear pulsed, along with anger.

She's more upset about the Agreement than she is about her own daughter nearly being killed.

First Mother waved an impatient hand. She'd heard the thought and dismissed it.

Resentment bubbled just beneath the surface. Betrayal joined it. The two festered and grew as Macari watched her mother turn and touch a stone pillar near the center of the gazebo. A pulse of power resounded through the court. Overhead, a bell rang. She'd summoned the Court. The full conclave. "Thank you for your report, daughter. Your mission is complete."

Macari glanced at her hand in time to see the symbol pulse a few times and then vanish.

"I suppose this means I'm not banished, then." Macari caressed the spot. She'd achieved her goal. But she didn't feel the relief she thought she'd feel. Nor the pride at having pleased her mother. Instead, sadness at the loss of something she couldn't identify enveloped her.

Macari stared at the ground. She spoke quickly, before the court members appeared. "You sent me on a mission that should have been impossible. It was a miracle that I crossed the Corsaerie into the Between. Even more that I received aid from a Fire Ancient. And to return took a sacrifice you couldn't possibly have anticipated. I ripped my soul apart. For you."

"Your actions were for the good of society." First Mother said stiffly.

Macari glanced up at her mother's frozen back. "What I'd like to know, Mother, is why? What could possibly make this insignificant information so valuable that you'd cast aside your only daughter to achieve it?"

"I sent an emissary of the Benata on a mission of gathering. Nothing more."

"Emissary." Macari repeated the word. It sounded cold. Heartless. The sort of word one might use to describe a bench or perhaps a spoon. An instrument, nothing more. Not daughter. A tool to be used.

Macari tried to make sense of the emotions she'd just gleaned from a woman who'd always been able to shield them. They'd always maintained some sort of natural immunity to each other's talents, before.

Now she realized there'd been nothing natural about it. When she opened the doors in her mind to release all the emotions she'd bottled up inside, it had allowed her to see who she really was. It had been her mother who taught her to do it. To deny her talent. To ignore herself, despite the damage it caused.

She never shielded her emotions from me. I did it myself. When

I didn't feel caring from my mother, I locked everything away. It hurt to admit.

First Mother now exuded anger, bitterness, intolerance. Panic and shame. It was the last emotion that took Macari by surprise. It wasn't shame at having sent her only daughter to be tortured. Macari searched a bit further.

She's ashamed of me. Or of herself.

The anger and panic stemmed from the final scene with Tarian. That was easy to see, here in the court building. It was also easy to sense the complete lack of concern for an only daughter, or even a citizen of the Benata, the society her mother claimed to love above all.

Macari probed into her mother's mind with abandon. She found no worry that a daughter might be injured. No outrage that she'd been abused. No sense of anything at all directed toward Macari herself other than shame.

Not even love.

Tears welled up as the thought struck and sadness stole Macari's heart. Now she knew why that door had been the last, and hardest, to open.

One by one court members entered the space, in mind and body. Their voices joined in the silence that had spun out between Macari and her mother.

The scenes Macari had shared with her mother replayed for all who entered, again and again. Each time, the fear and anger from First Mother increased, to the point Macari wondered if it would be wise to use her talent and siphon some of them away.

No. That's not who I am anymore. And it's not like it helped before. When the last of the gathering had entered, nearly fifty daemon crowded the space. First Mother commanded the center of the group. Macari remained seated on the bench. She ignored the glances and outright stares at her disheveled appearance and obvious bad manners.

Let them see. Let them all see the result of First Mother's actions.

Linked mind-to-mind, First Mother sent her thoughts to the Court, laced with a heavy dose of anger. *"As you have seen, the leader of the human society is with child. A child spawned from an act of Agreement that tilted the balance between the Mayfanata and Benata. Ruarc has betrayed society. He entered into Agreement with Tarian Xannon, human. He gave her the Book of Daemon in exchange for his seed within her."*

"The Book of Daemon?"

"Betrayal."

"He has breached Agreement."

"What is she doing with the Book?"

"What knowledge has been gleaned?"

"Has she used the information?"

Voices tumbled over themselves as the panic her mother felt spread through the group. Macari listened, amazed. Not one rational voice to break up the tirades.

Has no one noticed? Does the Court care what happened to me?

Her errant thought barely registered against the tide of outrage and frightened voices.

Her mother continued. *"He has created a child. His seed has entered the human plane. This cannot be allowed, for the good of society."*

Macari processed the thoughts, then jumped to her feet. "What do you mean, 'this'? What cannot be allowed, Mother?"

First Mother continued to address the crowd. *"A new mission shall begin. We must, for the good of society, remove the threat to Balance."*

"But how can we accomplish this?"

"Are they launching an attack on us?"

"Yes, the child must be dealt with."

"The child cannot be allowed."

First Mother held up a hand. Voices stilled as they waited for instructions.

"The child shall be destroyed, before birth. That would be easiest and best for society. If possible, this shall be done without harm to the mother."

The dubious tone that accompanied the word *if* left Macari with no doubt as to First Mother's real intentions. Kill the child, whatever the cost to whoever might be in the way. Including Tarian Xannon.

Macari couldn't stop herself. She stood on the bench next to her and used voice, rather than mind. "She's just a child. What possible harm could she cause? A child is future. And hope. It's an innocent!"

Macari stomped her foot, letting her frustration ripple into the assembled daemon. "It is not the Benata way to murder innocents. We have progressed beyond that horrible scene on the beach. Tell me we have, First Mother. Tell me we are not the kind of daemon who would slaughter even one child."

First Mother whipped around to face her daughter. In a few short strides she had crossed through the crowd and stood next to the bench. She thrust out a hand and grasped Macari's arm. She glared up at Macari as though seeing a stranger.

As she spoke, a command laced with power pressed into the skin. "You will honor the pact you've made with your blood line, with the Court, and with the office of First Mother. You will honor the vow you took to uphold the rule of this society. The child carried by Tarian Xannon must be destroyed. For the good of society. As the only daemon of the Court capable of reaching the human plane, I assign this task to you, First Daughter. Destroy the child. By whatever means necessary."

Macari gaped at her mother as the bond took hold and the mark of Air burned into the flesh on her arm.

"This you will do by the next moon cycle, or face..." First Mother paused, seeming to trip over her words. Her lips tightened into a tight white line. When she continued, the words were clipped and final. "If you do not complete this task, you will face banishment as is decreed by your oath. Such is my command and your mission." The crazed look on her mother's face wasn't far removed from the one Macari had seen on Preacher's.

Macari gaped at her mother, unable to speak. Wave after

wave of fear wrapped around the words blocked out all reason and logic. She'd never known her mother to act like this.

Stunned, all Macari could do was listen as her mother made plans she expected Macari to carry out on the human side.

CHAPTER TWENTY-FIVE

Macari watched court members leave, lost in thought. The meeting concluded; they'd stayed an unusual amount of time, discussing the possible ramifications of Tarian's child. After her short outburst and First Mother's mission assignment, no one had said a word to her or about her. They studiously pretended she didn't exist, except for the odd glance here and there.

Macari climbed down from the bench, numb. She walked slowly around the perimeter, breathing in the smell of roses, and waited for a moment alone with First Mother.

"You wish to speak?" First Mother waited at the arch.

Macari crossed the space to stand next to her mother. They remained under the influence of the gazebo, though obviously her mother wanted to leave.

It wouldn't matter, Mother. Thoughts or no thoughts, I'll always know how you feel.

First Mother clasped her hands tightly in front of her. Clearly, she was going to wait for Macari to speak her mind.

Fine.

Now that she had her mother alone, Macari struggled for words. She rubbed the mark on her arm for inspiration. She could feel it, a raised bubble of sore skin like a new scar. It made her neck twitch with every touch. She could still feel the burn of command in her veins. She could still see her mother's frantic eyes as she gave it. Words bubbled to the surface.

"How *could* you?"

First Mother raised an eyebrow.

"How could you send *anyone*, let alone your own daughter, to kill an unborn child? It's not the Benata way."

"For the good of society…" First Mother began.

Macari stomped her foot. "*I'm* society, Mother. And I'm a member of this Court. I'm your *daughter*, for star's sake. You would send your own daughter to commit a crime so horrible… that hasn't been….that…." Macari stuttered. Outrage boiled her words to a higher pitch. "And the mission you sent me on was *not* good for me."

For emphasis, Macari tugged at the tattered blouse, ripping a piece off it. She threw the scrap at her mother, who flinched but otherwise didn't react. "Do you understand what caused this? Do you *see* what happened to your daughter? To a member of your society?" She couldn't keep the scorn out of the word. Society had taken on a whole new meaning in the past few minutes. "Do you even care?"

First Mother's lips formed a tight line as though she could stop Macari's tirade or perhaps her own thoughts by keeping her mouth shut.

Macari waited, searching for any errant thought or emotion. *You feel nothing. Not one ounce of compassion. The one you fear showed far more concern for me. Is that what bothers you?*

No response.

She took a deep breath. "This new mission? What is it really about, Mother? Please. Make me understand why my life is worth this?"

First Mother's cold, dead eyes stared at Macari. When she finally spoke, her tone matched the empty expression of her eyes. "As a member of this Court you have the right to pose questions to the First Mother, of course. As First Mother, I have the right not to answer. However, I will tell you this. The good of the many *must* outweigh the good of a few. One sacrifice, or two, for the sake of society is a small price to pay for the security of thousands."

Again Macari sensed a flash of shame. She caught it, wondered at it, and tried to trace it to a thought. A reason. She found nothing but a wall.

"What have I ever done that caused you shame?" Macari whispered.

First Mother stiffened. She took two steps and exited the court, severing the mind link.

Macari called after her. "All this time, and you still don't understand that it's not a thought I receive from you. It's a lot deeper than that, and it's not a gift supplied by the Court."

Macari followed her mother. "I sense your emotions whether you want me to or not. In the court or out, it makes no difference. I sense all of it. It's a gift *you* gave me, by giving me life. You, and whatever male contributed."

Macari caught a flash of something at the word male. She'd never known the male figures who might have been considered her fathers. She'd never needed to. Since raising a daemon child happened in a communal manner she'd never lacked for guidance. Until now.

"I thought you blocked your emotions to protect me. But you didn't. You're ashamed of me. I've done everything you've ever asked without complaint. I ask again, Mother. What have I done to cause you shame?"

First Mother didn't turn to face her. She spoke over her shoulder, refusing to meet Macari's gaze. "You were born."

The words drifted away on the breeze, barely there.

Without another word, First Mother traveled, leaving Macari staring at an empty pathway.

CHAPTER TWENTY-SIX

Macari stood on her favorite hilltop overlooking Benata City and felt something she'd never felt toward her home before.

Disgust.

They wouldn't listen. They wouldn't see. It all boiled down to two sides of an argument that neither would let go and neither would win.

After her mother's abrupt departure, she'd sought out a few trusted members of the Court. All of them agreed with her mother, though none were as cold in the face of Macari's obvious distress. They all maintained that the human plane was a threat, that the child would destroy life as they knew it, would upset the Balance and perhaps destroy the planes. As a human with daemon essence and power, the child was an anomaly. Incredibly strong, even before birth. The best thing for society, they said, was to ensure she never grew to her potential. In that way, whatever

Ruarc planned would be thwarted. Killing an innocent child was a small price to pay. One child against the lives of all daemon was an easy choice to make, in their minds. First Mother said so, and they believed her.

Macari explained about the goodness in the House of Xannon. The rightness of utilizing all elements of magic. The strength that could come from combining forces with humans. The abilities. The hope. She expressed the idea that whatever Ruarc might have intended, this child would be raised by humans. She'd be influenced by Tarian Xannon, not Ruarc. The child would not be bound to any daemon court. She would not be obligated to act on Ruarc's behalf. She posed no obvious threat, now or in the future.

They responded to every one of her arguments with the same phrase. *The good of the many must outweigh the life of one.*

But to Macari, it felt weak and lopsided. Why couldn't they have both the one *and* the many? Why did they have to choose?

She'd seen enough on the Wind to know the human side, while it might have pockets of evil, also contained a lot of good. They carried with them traditions that must have been learned thousands of years ago, from daemon. And it wasn't like daemon hadn't perpetuated their share of evil as well. She'd seen that on the Wind, too. She'd seen the massacre at the hands of the Benata. Ironic that the event she witnessed with Serin and her village most likely spawned the very beginning of what became the House of Xannon. The overwhelming similarity in appearance spoke louder than words. Serin was ancestor to Tarian. Because they attacked, Serin had left her safe village and moved to a new home. She'd learned and lived and loved. And she'd left children to carry on after she'd gone. She'd left a legacy that included the Water Artifact. Because of that one horrible action on the beach, today a child with unlimited potential in her own right waited to be born and claim that same artifact.

Macari had given up trying to show them how foolish the actions had been, and how foolish the current plan most definitely was. She might be First Daughter, but she held no power and no sway with anyone in Court. Her mother's opinion and command were all that mattered.

At least, for now.

As First Daughter, she was bound by oath and magic to obey the commands of the First Mother, like all court members. She stood on the cliff, about to embark on a despicable mission set forth by a woman she thought she knew.

But I don't. I don't know you at all, do I Mother?

A sense of loss renewed itself deep in her heart. She stared at the Stulos and the Shee as they circled it. Tears worked their way out of her eyes and down her cheeks. She searched the feeling and finally gave it a name.

Betrayal.

How could you? Macari rubbed the mark of Air. *You send me to betray everything I've ever believed in. How could you do this to me?*

Her mother felt shame that Macari existed at all. *Why?* She'd always assumed her procreation happened in the usual way.

But it must have been unusual. Something about my birth causes you embarrassment and shame. Which means whoever you joined with causes the same. Who was he, Mother?

It was idle thought. She'd never know what male had mated with her mother. Not unless she somehow stumbled on it in the Wind. First Mother would never tell her.

I can't exactly go up to every daemon I see and ask. It doesn't matter anyway. If she made a mistake, it was hers. Not mine.

"Teigh trasna ort fein, Mother." She shouted the words. She liked the feel of it so much she screamed them again.

A high-pitched giggle near her ear startled her so much she jumped and swayed on the edge of the cliff.

You have changed, Wind Walker. You have grown. You see with new eyes.

"Much good it does me." Macari muttered, not willing to admit how much the Shee had scared her.

Jasmine giggled again. The giggle erupted into a cloud of feathers that soon formed the figure of a girl with white translucent hair.

Yes, much good it does. New eyes are needed for a journey to new places.

"But these new places bring pain, too."

Jasmine smiled. *"Sometimes pain is a journey. You will do well, Walker."*

"You can see that? Can you see how this turns out?"

Jasmine giggled, her form beginning to dissolve. *"None can see the future. But by judging the past, the future can be predicted."*

The girl disappeared, leaving only a few feathers floating on the breeze. Macari reached out and caught one.

"I predict you will thrive, Macari. I predict you will be needed. I predict you will be loved."

Jasmine giggled, a sound that evaporated even as the feather disappeared from Macari's hand.

She stared out at the valley, realizing that it might be the last time she stood on this hill. The last time she drank in the sun and the wind, the last time she felt the give and take of power. Sadness swept through her. She'd miss this place. If she didn't complete her mission, once again the threat of banishment hung over her head and heart. Once again, the mark burned vivid on her skin. Even now, the clock ticked.

She sent her sadness out into the breeze and let it sweep down to the city below. Then she stepped off the hill, and into the Wind.

CHAPTER TWENTY-SEVEN

A short stroll brought Macari to the center of a pleasant meadow lit by a sunless sky. She waited near the trees, knowing it wouldn't be long. Knowing it didn't matter if it was. Time meant nothing in the Between. And she wasn't in a hurry, anyway.

"Our Agreement is complete." The words, nearly a growl, came from the trees behind her.

She turned, and waited for Lasair to step closer. He didn't move from the shadows of the trees, but she saw his eyes sparking like small bonfires.

"Why didn't you just tell me how to bond? Why make it so difficult?"

Lasair stared at her but offered no explanation.

"You nearly got me killed. You know that? Why the games?"

"Fire rarely travels a straight line."

"Fire is chaos." Macari nodded. "It also causes quite a bit of destruction."

"Destruction is creation. Some barriers must be broken for Balance and life to grow."

"Whose life, Lasair? Yours? Serin's? What's your end game?"

Lasair worked his jaw. "You bear the mark yet again. Was your mission not successful?"

"You know it was. Too successful."

"I know only that the artifact has found a home."

"You can sense me as easily as I sense you." Macari crossed her arms, glaring at him. "Admit it."

"I admit nothing." Lasair blinked, and appeared before her. "You embark on a new mission. You wish a new Agreement?"

"You could just ask me why I'm here like a normal person." His eagerness, hidden under layers of masking gruffness, made her smile. "I don't seek Agreement with you, no. And yes, I have a new mission. I'm duty bound to obey."

"And yet, you rest Between." Lasair kept both hands at his side, one clenched in a fist, the other relaxed, but his eyes alert as they studied her face.

"I wished…I guess I wanted to thank you. For this." She patted her stomach where the artifact lay nestled against her skin. "I have a feeling I'll need it. I just…What's the answer, Lasair? My mission conflicts with what I know to be true. What my heart longs for. But if I do what I feel is right, I lose all that I have. All that I know."

"You seek advice."

"I guess I do."

"Ancient does not necessarily mean wise."

"Yet, you have more experience than I. Surely it counts for something?" She wanted to rant against him. Did he have to be so stoic? Couldn't he unbend and be a little more...human?

Lasair's lips twitched, and his eyes crinkled ever so slightly. "You may lose all that you know at this moment. But there is more to be learned. More to be lived. Follow what you know to be right and you will never lose what is most important." He pointed at her. "You."

"So you're saying sometimes bonds were made to be broken?"

"Perhaps, in the breaking, a new one may be created. Destruction *is* creation."

Beneath them, the ground shook. Macari stumbled, sidestepping to keep her balance. "What in stars is that?" She studied the ground as it buckled.

Lasair stared at the newly formed cracks in the ground that stretched out in front of them, looking thoughtful. A glimmer of a smile tugged at the corners of his mouth. His eyes flashed.

When he didn't answer, Macari grabbed his arm. He looked back at her then, one eyebrow raised.

"You know what that was."

Lasair inclined his head in a brief nod.

"What's happening?"

"Creation." Lasair's glanced down at her naval, where

the artifact lay embedded. Another flicker of a smile curved his lips.

"What's that supposed to mean?"

Lasair offered her a brief dip of his head, and turned to leave. He paused and looked back over his shoulder. "Will you do as commanded?"

She glanced at the mark on her arm, still vivid. *I don't know.*

Lasair turned his back, walking quickly away. "You do not belong here."

She watched him go. *Yeah, well, neither do you.*

"You didn't answer the question!" She shouted the words, but they were lost in the rumble of quaking ground.

Faced with an empty meadow and ground that refused to stay still, Macari took the Corsaerie. Once there, she rested on the outer edge, trying to decide what to do. *Whatever caused the ground to shake must have been important. Lasair liked it. More than that. He was hopeful.*

Her initial instinct was to report the incident to First Mother. But she'd been commanded to go to the human plane and destroy an unborn child. First Mother wouldn't care about a little shaking ground. In fact, it might send her into even more of a frenzy. She'd insist Macari act as soon as possible, maybe even move up the timeline. *And if I don't do as she says, I'll be banished from my home forever.*

And if I do, what becomes of me? What kind of daemon will I be?

She thought of Alex. Anna. Tarian. The energy of The Edge. The beauty of the island and black sand. Even the hated water. It concealed Ancients who'd saved her life though they'd had no reason to act other than kindness. Banishment didn't sound half bad, anymore.

Something shimmered on the Wind in front of her, an anomaly that caught her attention immediately. A window formed, and within she saw two Balance Court members with their colorful hair and pure white eyes. They gestured as one, beckoning.

"Naoise Sha'Macariah, Keeper of the Fire Artifact, you are summoned to the Balance Court."

As the binding settled around her and she felt the compulsion take hold, Macari grinned. She had a feeling she was about to find out what had caused the ground to shake. *Bet something huge has happened. Something that made Lasair very happy.*

A glimmer of hope sparked in the pit of her stomach. They'd called her Keeper. Like Tarian. *Wonder how Mother will react to that?*

She'd have to put up the strongest mental shields she'd ever used before she appeared at the Balance Court next to her mother. If she was going to defy her mother's command, she didn't want to leak that knowledge ahead of time. She focused on that, and then on placing false memories and thoughts woven in between more shields to hide her visit with Lasair and her intentions.

When she finished, she'd created a maze so complicated it would take her mother years to sort through it. She laughed, delighted. She'd found a spark of hope among humans, on a plane with very little magic. She could help fan that spark into a flame. *First Mother wouldn't know hope if she were painted with it and set on fire.*

Macari pulled on the Air around her to create a hooded robe. After she covered herself, she paused in front of the window. She grinned at the welcoming pair from the Balance Court within it.

"Let the games begin."

<<<<>>>

REVIEW TIME!

I hope you enjoyed this story and that it took you away, if only for a short while, from the day to day stuff life heaps on us. The best way to ensure that authors continue to provide fun escapes is by leaving honest reviews at your vendors of choice. Your opinions matter to others who are trying to decide what to read. And they make authors do happy dances.

Sign up for the newsletter at <u>melindavan.com</u> and get the inside scoop, extra scenes, plus images which inspired the stories.

MORE IN THE HOUSE OF XANNON

PROMISE OF MAGIC

Some promises are deadly to keep.

TAKING EARTH

The whole world can change in 24 hours.

ELEMENTS OF MAGIC

Balance is hard, and sometimes deadly.